Green Peace

Green Peace

By Joyce Cooper

Transcribed from the original manuscript

by Guy Beauchamp.

Proof read by Annie Beauchamp.

Published by Joyce Cooper Publishing
First edition December 25th 2014

ISBN 978-0-9928735-3-0

Joyce Cooper Publishing
Grange Hall Cottage
Kildwick
Keighley
BD20 9AD

Dedication

To Troy with love

and

the hope that your Green Rabbit will understand!

Preface

We now live in a world where anyone can publish a book they have written (and re-written) using their personal computer and researched on the internet. Technology is giving writers a golden age.

This was not the case when Joyce wrote this book in the 1970s...all she had was a typewriter, a clear and magical vision, and a lively, highly intelligent and funny mind. Just reading it brought back great memories of sunny summers and Joyce reading the latest installment of Green Peace hot off the type-writer in the cool of the evening. The book meant a great deal to Joyce and getting published would have delighted her – and perhaps the manner of its publishing might have amused her as well...

It wasn't easy publishing this book: There was only a hardcopy manuscript to work from with hand-written amendments and it was not always clear. So there may be errors – sorry! – and there are some strange turns of phrase from the time it was written. Where possible I have left all of these in and changed as little as possible to produce it as Joyce intended.

Annie has done a great job of proof reading but I have amended it since so any errors remaining are (of course!) mine.

Finally, the book achieved something quite astounding for me as the last paragraph (which I won't reveal and don't sneak a peak!) both ended the story and awoke something in me that had been sleeping...that (green?) "something" has stayed with me ... and I am all the more happy for that!

Guy Beauchamp.

Contents

Part I – Midsummer Eve

A Sabbatical is a time of refreshment
A Rabbittical is the refreshment of time
Book of Proverbs (G-R-A-V)

Glossary

G-R-A-S-S Green Rabbit Automatic Sixth Sense
G-R-I-L Green Rabbit Instant Logic
G-R-I-D Green Rabbit Instant Desire
G-R-I-P Green Rabbit Instant Proverbs
G-R-I-H Green Rabbit Instant Hunch
G-R-A-N-D Green Rabbit Approved 'N Desired
G-R-I-M Green Rabbit Instant Madness
G-R-I-P-E Green Rabbit Instant Painless Educator
B. O. P. (G-R-A-V) Book Of Proverbs (Green Rabbits Approved Version) Books 1-3

There is no copyright restriction on substituting H(uman) for G-R on all cases

Chapter 1

A world's end is an on-going situation
(B. O. P. Bk. 1)

The ball was dead on target and the little signpost, rising like some cubist flower from its sheath of hog-weed and tall grass, quivered under the attack. Well pleased with his aim, Sergei ran at the ball ready to catch it, but it was not to be. He could only watch, in still silence, as a part of apparently green and furry arms stretched up out the long grass and caught it. The ball was then thrown up again and kicked, by an apparently green, furry leg of giant proportions, in a great arc. It went hurtling down the road to where Dasha was ambling along, humming her favourite Top-Of-The-Pops and twirling a buttercup.

She screamed out, "Hey, watch it!" at the same moment the owner of the green limbs chose to reveal him... her... itself.

"That was not a friendly act!" Itself pronounced solemnly. "You came close to implanting my face as a permanent feature on this signpost."

"I'm... I'm... I'm sorry," Sergei stuttered. "I didn't know... I didn't see you... I didn't know anybody was there." But whether his embarrassment stemmed from his thoughtless shot, or the fact that he was apparently address a five-foot green rabbit, Sergei would not, at that moment, have been able to say.

"Well, no matter," Itself declared briskly, "no bones broken. But now that we are acquainted, perhaps you could render me a small service?"

"If I can help you, of course I will." Sergei's answer was no more than a polite reflex in an irrational situation.

Then Itself smiled. Something emanated from the dark rabbit eyes which softened Sergei's confusion. "Thank you so much, but first let me introduce myself. Due to a small problem, of which you may care to hear later, I call myself Middlesex!"

"Er... how do you do, Mr Middlesex," Sergei responded uncertainly. "I am Sergei, and this," he turned and waved Dasha on urgently, "and this is my twin sister Dasha."

"Delighted to meet you," Middlesex beamed at Dasha. The dark eyes were tranquil and inviting as the waters of a lagoon. "It is indeed an ill wind that blows no good. If your brother's ball had gone wide of the mark and not roused me, we might have passed each other like ships in the night." The dark eyes were compelling. "And that, I am beginning to sense, would have been to our mutual loss."

"I guess so," Dasha replied, bewildered by the words as much as by Middlesex's appearance. "What did you say your name was?"

Middlesex glowed a little greener, straightened the floppy ears, and twirled the silver and ebony walking stick in a green paw.

"I go by the name of Middlesex, and I am the founder member of the R.A.C." As if in confirmation, the medallion which dangled from a silver chain on the green furred chest was held forward.

"R.A.C.?" Sergei looked puzzled. "But that's the badge of the Royal Automobile..."

Middlesex broke in firmly. "No, you are mistaken! This is the chain of office of the founder member of the Rabbit Aristocratic Club, which happens to be me. In fact I am the only member of whose existence I am aware. But come, you said you would help me."

"Let's sit down," Dasha said suddenly. "There's a lot to think about," and she flopped down in the hedgerow among the scabious and scarlet pimpernel.

"Yes, let us relax and get to know each other properly," Middlesex agreed. "Besides, it will enable us to lay out my map fully."

The twins watched in amazement as an Ordinance Survey Map of the west coast of Scotland and the Isle of Skye was laid out on the grass.

"Now!" said Middlesex, "let us consider this signpost."

The twins looked up at it as though for the first time. It bore the simple legend: BY ROAD.

"Well," said Sergei, "what about it?"

"Now, perhaps you could help me find this elusive place of BY ROAD on my map. Wherever I travel, there are always roads which lead there, but I have never managed to arrive."

Sergei and Dasha began to giggle.

"There's no such place, and this is Suffolk, not Scotland," Dasha explained, trying to hide her amusement.

"And this road doesn't go anywhere," Sergei added.

"That is plainly nonsense, " Middlesex retorted. "A map is a map, and all roads go somewhere! It was once said that all roads led to Rome, but in this modern world it would seem that Rome has been superseded. It is obvious that in this twentieth century the acme of perfection lies in BY ROAD!"

"What we mean," Sergei parried, "is that it just goes up to our house and then peters out on an old airfield!"

"Then you live in BY ROAD!" Middlesex was triumphant. "And, as I know only too well, there are roads all over the country leading to your house, you must be very important and worthwhile people."

"Of course we're not!" Dasha was getting a little impatient. "I tell you BY ROAD just means...well, a little road that's not often used. "

"Quite, quite!" Middlesex agreed quickly, tapping a green paw on one side of a squat nose with a conspiratorial air. "You may rest assured that your secret is safe with me. However, G-R-I-L advises me that I have, at last, found a suitable base for that which must be done to further the cause of R.A.C."

"You talk in riddles," Sergei complained. "What did you say advises you?"

"Why, G-R-I-L of course. Green Rabbit Instant Logic. You see, always think in capitals, it disciplines the mind to concentrate on the important things in life."

To Sergei, this sounded suspiciously like the "uplifting" messages frequently handed out at school assemblies and, in schoolboy fashion, he instantly rebelled against it.

"What do you think the important things in life are, Mr Middlesex?" he asked mockingly. "Neat rows of Cos lettuces, all ready for the nibbling?"

Middlesex regarded him sadly, and by-passed the hostility. "Too much quality and very poor quality for my taste. I prefer the open, crinkled variety myself. And please, no handle to my name – just plain Middlesex which, in a way, highlights the purpose of my quest."

His quiet dignity appealed to Dasha, who had been embarrassed by her brother's rudeness. "What is a quest?" She asked politely. "Didn't knights go on them or something?"

"Indeed they did," Middlesex agreed. "You see, a quest is a search of a very personal nature: looking for something about which you know very little."

"And what are you questing for?" demanded a slightly abashed, but still sceptical, Sergei.

"Me! I am searching for *me*," Middlesex answered simply. "You see, I know nothing about me. I have no idea where I came from or where I am going; who I am or what I am. I don't even know whether I am a buck or doe; hence the name, Middlesex, which I have chosen for myself."

"I can tell you what you are," Sergei parried. "You're a big green rabbit and, what was it you said, something about belonging to the Rabbit Aristocracy Club?"

"Ah, yes, indeed!" Middlesex sighed. "That I am an aristocrat among my breed, is all that I do know with any degree of certainty."

"How on earth can you say that?" Sergei was relentless.

"By the wisdom of G-R-I-L, what else?" Middlesex answered a little sharply. "Is it not a fact that human aristocrats are said to be 'blue blooded' ?"

"Yes, but that doesn't mean that they're bl..." Sergei began, but Middlesex cut him short.

"Therefore, by the application of G-R-I-L, it is obvious that I am, as you might say, green-blooded. This phenomenon sets me apart from the ordinary strain of *Lupus Cuniculus*, and implies the existence of *Lupus Arististocratus!*"

Sergei burst out laughing. Middlesex had completely disarmed him.

"Q. E. D.!" he shouted. "I like your logic."

"You, too, think in capitals," Middlesex grinned. "Capital! I knew we would understand one another. But what does this Q. E. D. stand for?"

"*Quad erat demanstrandum,*" Dasha answered bravely. "And that's all the Latin I know. It means *it is proven.*"

"Excellent! Capital!" Middlesex cried. "We shall be friends. Q. E. D. We have proved ourselves. Give your paws and we will shake on it. Then, if you will, you shall take me to BY ROAD."

"OK. It's obviously useless to argue with G-R-I-L," Sergei conceded, taking Middlesex's paw.

"Even if we wanted to,"" Dasha added laughing, shaking Middlesex's other paw. "Which we don't, it's too much F. U. N.!"

"Capital! Capital!" Middlesex shouted, throwing the discarded map over the hedge and, twirling the silver and ebony stick in the style of a Major Domo, set off up the lane. "My G-R-I-Hs – that is to say my Green Rabbit Instant Hunches, not be confused with haunches – have never let me down yet."

The twins followed their new F-R-I-E-N-D, Dasha playing an imaginary penny whistle and Sergei banging on a big bass drum. The lane narrowed as it came to a white, cross-barred gate, beyond which Mrs Polenski was on her knees weeding the rose bed. She sat back on her heels and looked up towards the approaching hullaballoo. She watched the arrival of the little procession with more than ordinary interest, curious at the authenticity of the rabbit costume.

Middlesex stopped at the gate and waved reverently at the large Elizabethan cottage, at the uneven white walls and thatched roof which sported ornate, twisted brick chimneys. In the garden the old well, its roller and winding handle still shakily erect over the concrete slab which lay across the top, completed the composition. The whole was framed by olive green willow trees along two sides, and a tangled hedge of hazel, bramble and dogrose, which sheltered the back of the cottage. Lastly, solemnly, he regarded the name painted on the white gate. Fortunately it was all in capitals: WORLD'S END.

Turning to the twins, the greenness of Itself dazzled their eyes. "I knew it! I knew it!" Middlesex was ecstatic. "My G-R-I-Hs have never let me down, BY ROAD leads to WORLD'S END! To where else could it lead? And G-R-I-L shows us that all ends are but new beginnings. I pronounce this place G-R-A-N-D, that is to say – Green Rabbit Approved N'Desired!" .

"I'm glad you like it," Dasha said lamely, overwhelmed by the enthusiasm of Middlesex.

Sergei swung back the gate. "Come in and meet Mum. Her eyes are nearly popping out of her head."

"Mum, this is Middlesex," Dasha shouted as she ran up the path, "who is going to stay with us."

Middlesex beamed at Mrs Polenski, stopped, and with both paws clasped over the top of his ebony stick, bowed politely and said, "I am enchanted to meet you, Mrs Mum! I do hope that we shall be friends; but I am sure, that as the mother of these three charming children, it is a foregone conclusion."

Mrs Polenski was in too great a state of shock to react other than normally. "How do you do, Mr Middlesex," she said in her best 'the-vicar-has-come-to-tea' voice. "Won't you please sit down?," and she waved vaguely in the direction of the non-existent chairs.

"Just 'Middlesex', please," Itself corrected her, sitting down obligingly on the grass.

Mrs Polenski followed the example and turned to Dasha to ask for her invariable antidote to profound shock. "Make a cup of tea, will you, dear? I'm sure Mr …I beg your pardon, Middlesex would welcome a drink. It really has turned out very warm."

But Dasha was too excited to be despatched on any such errand.

"In a minute, Mum," she said impatiently. "Listen! We met Middlesex at the turning. Sergei nearly flattened…" and so the whole story poured forth from the twins non-stop, one carrying on when the other had run out of breath.

Middlesex, meanwhile, gazed around, beaming contentedly and murmuring over and over again "Capital, capital! Just capital!"

"…So here we are, and Middlesex is going to stay with us,"Sergei at last concluded the saga.

"Yes, yes, I see," Mrs Polenski murmured vaguely. "At least, I think I see…But please, Dasha, what about that cup of tea? I really can't think without something to give me strength.."

"But Middlesex can stay, right?" Sergei urged impatiently.

"Why I … I shall have to think about it, I suppose.." But then her gaze met that of Middlesex, and a sensation of cool velvet flowed around her being and she began to calm down. Her mind was slowly coming into focus again. "A green rabbit," went her thoughts in slow motion, "a green rabbit who can talk; a green rabbit who can talk and whom we can all see and hear." Then she remembered how the twins had talked of the problems of identity – the quest. "So!" her mind went on, "A green rabbit who can talk and we can all see and hear, and who has identity problems! No, I can't pass up this opportunity to observe the condition at first had. Much better than books!" And so, as she had accepted the fact that she was not dreaming, the conviction that Middlesex must stay, however bizarre the whole affair appeared, crystallised in her mind. She straight into those darkly velvet eyes again, and suddenly, everything seemed quite normal.

"But of course Middlesex will stay," she said briskly, and, as the twins ran off to put the kettle on, they heard their mother saying, "Now does it worry you much, to know so little about yourself?" They looked at each other and dissolved in to giggles.

"I think Mum's met her match at last," Sergei said. Their mother's dabbling in psychology alternately amused and irritated her offspring.

As they drank their tea, the conversation turned once more to mundane matters. "I hope you won't mind if your bedroom is in the attic," Mrs Polenski asked. "It's a very pleasant room, and the view is delightful."

"Capital, Mrs Mum," Middlesex was enthusiastic. "A room with a view is very conducive to the functioning of G-R-I-P-E."

"Which is?" Sergei demanded, now thoroughly at home with Middlesex's way of thinking.

"Green Rabbit Instant Painless Educator – what else?"

"What else!" Laughed Sergei. "Come on, we'll show you your room."

That evening, after tea, the twins took Middlesex on a tour of inspection, ending up at the disused Second World War airfield that still stretched its runways through fields of ripening corn.

"This is where our grandfather flew from," Sergei explained. "He was Polish, you see, and when the Germans invaded Poland in '39 he managed to get away to come to England and join the R. A. F."

"He's dead now," said Dasha, "but that's why we've got such funny names. Sergei was his name and Dasha my Gran's. Silly, really!"

"There are compensations," Middlesex argued, "to knowing who and what you are. I have been searching a long time to know just who and what I am."

"How long has it been?" Sergei was sympathetic.

Middlesex shrugged. "Who knows even that? I don't even know how old I am or who my parents were. Still, that is always difficult for a rabbit, you know!" Suddenly, the green fur took on a brighter glow. "But G-R-A-S-S tells me that here, at WORLD'S

END, I shall find some answers. On the other paw, G-R-I-L warns also that to know one's age, sex and class can be limiting factors."

"I don't think it limits me to know that I'm a twelve-year old boy," Sergei laughed, "and I'm Class 4 Alpha!"

"Maybe you don't!" Dasha parried. "Anyway, here we are."

Middlesex stopped. "What is this sad ruin of a place?"

They were standing before a long, dilapidated concrete hut, with broken windows and a leaky, corrugated-asbestos roof.

"This is where the air-crews lived," Sergei answered. "Some people say they are haunted by all the men who didn't come back from missions."

"Do you believe in ghosts?" Middlesex wanted to know.

"'Course not!" Sergei retorted too confidently. "I want to come up here one night, but Dasha's too scared." There was an expectant pause as Sergei struggled with his sense of fairness. "And I'm too scared to come on my own," he finally admitted. Then inspiration struck: "I say, Middlesex, would you come up with me one night?"

Middlesex's eyes closed for a long minute; the twins waited, and only the distant grumble of grouse echoed in the still air. Then the great eyes opened slowly. "You have aroused G-R-A-C, that is to say my Green Rabbit Active Curiosity. Yes, I will accompany you. And why not tonight? It is the time of the late moon if I'm not mistaken."

"If you'll come, I shall come too," Dasha said decisively. "At least I know you wouldn't run off and leave me, or do something stupid!"

"That's great!" Sergei shouted. "We'll put new batteries on the torches and be up here on the stroke of midnight."

"Then we had better retire to sleep early," suggested Middlesex.

"We can't do that," Sergei protested. "We'd never wake up again."

"But I will," said Middlesex calmly. "I am nocturnal by nature, and will therefore find no difficulty in waking when the restless ambition of your world sleeps."

"Aren't you afraid if you're out all night?" Dasha asked.

"The night is a friend," Middlesex explained softly. "Even old Bill Shakespeare had it wrong when talked of the night as a time of evil. No great and bloody battles have ever been fought at night, you know."

"The great bomber raids were nearly all at night" Sergei argued.

"Those were not battles," Middlesex said sadly, "they were massacres. No, the honourable contests between equals, as when young knights clad in Spitfire and Messerschmitt fought each other, were daytime happenings!"

There was a brief, pregnant pause before Middlesex continued. "But when your species would break the natural law, it does so in the darkness, ashamed of its own vulgarity. Only we, who live by the natural law, do not abuse the darkness and the night."

The twins were silent, not fully understanding, yet precociously aware. Middlesex looked at the two youngsters: innocent yet, but already trapped in the human condition. Then compassion possessed the Green Rabbit – the compassion of the hunted for the hunter.

"And that's enough of that!" Itself said briskly. "I shall wake you at 23:30 hours, as our R. A. F. friends would say."

"Synchronise your watches, gentlemen," Sergei shouted, with a great sense of relief. "I'll race you both home!" and he went hurtling back down the runway towards WORLD'S END. Dasha hesitated briefly, smiled shyly at Middlesex and then ran after Sergei. Middlesex played hide-and-seek leapfrog with them – first in front and then behind, so that they reached home breathless and merry again.

Mrs Polenski did not show, if indeed she felt, any suspicions when the children volunteered for bed at 22:00 hours. Nevertheless, their request for new torch batteries did cause a momentary flutter of curiosity, but it passed quickly. The book which she had been immersed when they had burst in, on research into animal language with special references to the dolphin, was of far more immediate interest. But she, too, went to bed early. Stephan was due home in the early hours from the Tehran run, and she needed her sleep for the few hectic days ahead when he was at home.

So a profound peace and stillness settled over the cottage as the busy, but quieter, inhabitants of Planet Earth had their day.

Chapter II

Lack of vision is the forcing ground of fear
(B. O. P. Bk. 3)

Middlesex crept from bedroom to bedroom and prodded the twins with the silver and ebony stick at precisely 23:30 hours. Sleepily, they emerged from under the bedclothes fully dressed, and put on their plimsolls. Then, clutching torches, they tip-toed out into the scented June night. It was much darker than Sergei had expected and Dasha had feared. As their eyes adjusted to the darkness, they saw a green glow that seemed to emanate from Middlesex's fur and, in the glow, their fears evaporated.

"I shall lead the way, using G-R-A-S-S," Middlesex said quietly. "Follow me closely, in Indian file, and you won't need your torches.."

"What's G-R-A-S-S again?" Dasha asked, sandwiched between Middlesex and Sergei.

"G-R-A-S-S is Green Rabbit Automatic Sixth Sense, what else?" Middlesex laughed. "Similar but, of course, superior to Human RADAR!"

"But of course!" Sergei mimicked, giggling.

"Naturally," said Middlesex. "And, if you apply G-R-I-L, you will appreciate that as the majority of human inventions are but attempts to imitate nature, they rarely match the original in scope, flexibility or reliability. G-R-A-S-S leads me safely through night fields and human relationships. Furthermore, G-R-A-S-S is fool-proof; RADAR is not!"

Sergei was irrepressible. "No," he giggled, "I suppose nothing would fool you in to thinking that a flock of flying geese were enemy missiles?"

The green glow grew a little brighter as Middlesex chalked up another victory for G-R-I-L.

"I think we're almost there," Dash whispered apprehensively.

"Yes, we are," Middlesex confirmed. "And don't be frightened by all the scurrying and scampering, it's only rabbits and mice and suchlike, who just want to be left alone." And Middlesex's ears, usually carried at a relaxed droopy angle, were now pointed and alert.

They had reached the half-open door hanging crazily on its hinges. Middlesex pushed it with the tip of the ebony stick and it creaked wider. There was much frenzied activity from the night visitors, as the twins' torches swept floor and walls clean of darkness, only for it to tumble back seconds later as the pencil beams moved on. Old cans, twisted bars of metal, fragments of wood with jagged edges were etched black and tungsten-hard in the mini-floodlights, throwing grotesque shadow shapes that danced with the slow distortion of mirrors at a fair.

"It's spooky," Dasha whispered.

"Weird, real weird," Sergei added.

"There is nothing here that is not ordinary and ugly in the full light of day," Middlesex said in a normal voice. "It is only the reality of the another world, that occupies the same space-time continuum as the one which you are familiar, that transposes this rubble in to the supernatural."

"How can you be so unromantic?" Dasha complained.

"You've been reading too much sci-fi," Sergei teased.

"Neither accusation is valid," Middlesex retorted. "I admit I find it fascinating, but the perception which G-R-A-S-S and G-R-I-L afford me grants me vision that is not obscured by primeval fear. It also suggests we are looking for the wrong thing!"

"Then what should we be-" Dash began to ask, only to be interrupted by a loud cry from Sergei. He had been walking round the room, examining the walls closely with his torch, while Middlesex spouted philosophy. "Hey, come here, you two!" He waved his torch. "Look what I've found!"

Dasha and Middlesex looked and, plainly etched on the dirty whitened walls, they saw an enormous rabbit, standing erect on its haunches. A large speech balloon issued from its mouth like a giant hiccough.

"Gosh! What is it saying?" Dasha shouted, all hushed reverence for the witching hour now gone. She peered at the scrawl by the light of her torch, gently easing away some spider-thread festooned with dead leaves and dust. "Run…run rabbit, run-run-run…and then something about his gun, and don't be a rabbit pie!"

"Revolting!" Middlesex commented. "But lend me your torch, please," Itself walked along the wall, peering closely. "This is most interesting! Capital, capital! Here, you see, we have veritable army of bunnies under the surveillance of a leader who is great stature, stands erect and has the power of human speech!"

Dasha laughed. "Don't you mind being called a bunny? I would have thought that you hated it."

"And so I should," Middlesex responded uncompromisingly. "I am not a bunny! That is the name reserved for the wild brown members of our species – the kind brought by The Conqueror to feed his Anglo-Saxon serfs, while he and his cronies ate their *mouton* and *boeuf* and *porc*. Even the name 'rabbit' is old French from *rabotte*; 'bunny' is a later unspeakable corruption, but I am an indigenous Rabbit, an indigenous Green Rabbit."

"And founder member of thc R.A.C.! Here endeth the first lesson. Yeah, sure, we know," Sergei goaded.

"That is so," Middlesex said, in a tone of hurt dignity. "And here we have pictorial proof that what G-R-A-S-S advocates instinctively, and G-R-I-L deduces, is the Truth!"

"I'm sorry," Sergei apologised, suddenly ashamed of his rudeness. "I didn't mean to hurt your feelings, but you do get on your high horse a bit at times, you know."

"Rabbits, even Green Rabbits," said Middlesex still smarting under Sergei's attack, "do not, to my knowledge, ride horses. But I might try it sometime, at that!" Itself added with a chuckle.

"Sergei means you sound a bit… a bit *pompous* at times, Middlesex." Dasha added quickly, pouring oil on troubled waters. "But please don't be cross, because he really is sorry if he's been rude, aren't you Sergei?"

Sergei held out his hand. "Sorry, Middlesex. P-A-X?"

"P-A-X?"

"Peace," said Sergei. "The hand of friendship, and I promise not to tease you again."

Middlesex beamed. "P-A-X: And the paw of friendship on it. I think my sense of humour must be slipping.."

"Now, can we get back to this?" Dasha asked, waving her torch to the wall. "Of what truth is it the proof?"

"Well," said Middlesex, "I expect you have seen photographs of the cave paintings done by the early members of your species?"

The twins nodded.

"Then here," said Middlesex, "is a latter day example. Here we have a large upright rabbit, which could only have been a Green Rabbit, warning the bunnies of danger, and they are obeying him.." Itself peered closer. "In fact, there are traces of green on the drawing.." The darkness shielded the awkwardness of the presence of dry green rivulets down the wall. "It must have been a memorable occasion indeed."

"You mean that you think this was drawn by a pre-historic rabbit?" Sergei asked.

"No, no," said Middlesex patiently. "This was drawn by a relatively modern human – even your grandfather, perhaps! But, whoever, he was a privileged human for he know of the existence of Green Rabbits. Otherwise, why the size, the upright position and the speech balloon?"

"I suppose it could be," Sergei said doubtfully, at the mercy of G-R-I-L.

"And most assuredly is," Middlesex asserted. "Perhaps you did not observe that the rabbit has a medallion around his neck like me. But the capitals are different. Come here, look! R.A.A.F."

"Oh yes, there were Aussies here too," Sergei said. "That means Royal Aust…" and stopped tactfully as Dasha's toe connected painfully with his shin bone.

"That is correct," Middlesex agreed, choosing to ignore Sergei's interpretation. "Rabbit Aristocratic Air Force. I wouldn't mind betting that prior to RADAR, any pilot or squadron which had secured the co-operation of a Green Rabbit were highly successful against the enemy. This drawing may indeed be a symbolic representation of such a partnership."

"I still say-" Sergei began again.

"Shut up!" said Dasha furiously.

"Sh, sh!" Middlesex said suddenly. "Put out your torches!"

In the darkness Middlesex glowed greenly again.

"What is it?" Dasha whispered.

"Someone coming – near the hangar," Middlesex whispered back.

They waited. Dasha and Sergei could hear nothing but the pounding of their own hearts. Through one of the broken windows they could see a pencil beam of light coming towards the hut.

"Come on," whispered Sergei urgently, "Let's make a dash for it.." He grabbed Dasha by the hand and pulled her unwillingly form the hut. Once outside, panic seized them both and they ran madly in the vague direction of WORLD'S END.

Middlesex, however, did not follow them, hiding instead behind the open door. The whole hut was bathed in an eerie green light, so that now the tangle of rubble took on the character of a looming space monster. As the light outside drew nearer, the footsteps slowed down. They came to a slow halt a few yards away, and tapped of a message of uncertainty.

A moment's pause, then, "Come out now! This is the Police. No nonsense, mind you!"

Middlesex grinned and glowed more greenly. There were two faltering steps forward.

"Come out, I tell you! Or we'll come in and get you."

Middlesex kicked some pebbles across the floor.

"There is someone in there, Bill!" Then is sharp official tones, "Come on, out you come. We just want to know who you are, and what you're doing up here at this time of night."

Silence! A deep, provocative silence!

"Right then, we're coming in," and the footsteps advanced. But halfway through the door, they stopped.

"There's a peculiar green light in here!"

"That's odd – very odd! Can you see where it's coming from, Ted?" The voice was apprehensive.

A torch beam swept quickly round the room. "I can't see what can be making it. There's no-one in here. I don't like the look of this at all."

"Put your torch out again, Ted." And the green glow returned more intense and quivering, as Middlesex shook with silent laughter. A pawful of pebbles hit the roof and cascaded noisily down.

There was a nervous cough. "I don't think there's anyone here, Bill. It must just be rats or something."

"I think you're right, Ted. Must be something reflecting. We'd better get back to the car. Sarge'll be wondering where we've got to."

As a *coup de grace*, Middlesex gave the wall a smart kick with a powerful hind leg and the door rattled and groaned. The two policemen took one last, quick look at the green glow, and hastily departed. They did not run, however, for even at one o'clock in the morning in the middle of nowhere, the dignity of their lawful calling sustained them. They switched on their powerful torches and proceeded in an orderly fashion down the rutted, grass-invaded runway. At about fifty yards distance, P.C. Bill made the mistake of turning to look back at the hut, where his eye was caught by a large green glow moving swiftly through the corn. He grabbed his companion's arm: "Put your torch out," he hissed "and look at that!"

The two policemen watched the green glow moving along a diagonal path, in what they could only later describe as 'bunny-hops'.

"Come on, Bill, let's get it!" P.C. Ted shouted suddenly, and so the two men plunged in to the corn.

The green glow led them backwards, forwards, round in circles; played hide-and-seek round the hanger and then back in to the waist-high corn. Sometimes it let them get near; at other times it would disappear and appear hundreds of yards away. They spread out, lost each other and panicked, using their torches to find each other again. After nearly an hour of this, they were exhausted and paths of broken corn testified to their crazy chase. Then they saw the green glow going in to the garden of WORLD'S END. They used their last reserves of wind and energy to charge through the hedge, oblivious to all to the bramble attack on hands, faces, and clothes. Two minutes later the cottage lay before them, dark and silent, with not a flicker of green to be seen. The two men stared up at the uncommunicative wisdom, and wondered what they should do next.

"I think we'd better rouse Mrs Polenski and... and..." said P.C. Bill.

"And what?" P.C. Ted demanded. "Tell here there are fairies at the bottom of her garden?"

"Well... we can at least warn her that there's something suspicious going on."

Their dilemma solved itself. An upstairs light came on; then the window opened and Mrs Polenski leaned out.

"Is that you, Stephan?" she called in a sleepy voice.

Ted cleared his throat. "No, Mrs Polenski. It's the Police: Constable Plunkett and I."

"Oh no! Something's happened! What is it? Has Stephan had an accident? Wait, I'm coming down," and the rising pitch of her voice had hardly died away, before the hall light went on and the front door opened.

"Come in, please come in. What has happened?"

"It's alright, Mrs Polenski," P.C. Plunkett said in a warm and reassuring tone. "Nothing has happened to anyone. It's alright, really! Nothing terrible has happened."

"Then... then what...?"

"Perhaps we could all go in and sit down? It's a long story," P.C. Wimble suggested, as he had the sudden conviction that his legs were about to buckle under him, and as he became aware of just how much his hands and face were hurting.

"You're not hiding anything from me, you're sure?" Mrs Polenski persisted as she led the way in to the sitting room. "No accident, honestly?"

"Absolutely nothing," P.C. Wimble re-iterated firmly as, with a great sigh of relief, he flopped down onto the settee.

"That's right!" P.C. Plunkett added. "We were just chasing something and it came this way, in to your garden – and a merry chase it was!"

Mrs Polenski looked at the two shattered arms of the law and, as a suspicion grew in her mind, pity replaced anxiety.

"I'll make you some coffee, and bring something for those cuts and scratches," she said with concern. Then, after putting on the kettle she crept upstairs to the twins' bedrooms. They appeared to be fast asleep, so she went to Middlesex's room and peeped nervously round the door. A green head glowed on the pillow, admitting gentle snores. Later, as she listened to the incredible story the two policemen related, she had occasion to remember that green glow!

When she returned to the sitting room with the coffee, hot water, cotton wool and Germolene, P.C. Ted was sprawled back on the settee and saying "It's beginning to seem like a bad dream, except for my face. Those brambles are wicked."

P.C. Bill was sitting uneasily on the edge of the chair. "How are we going to tell all this to the Sarge?" he was moaning unhappily. "He'll laugh us out of court, then eat us for breakfast.."

Mrs Polenski poured the coffee. "Now, tell me all about it," she said gently.

And tell her they did, step by step and glow by glow. It was nearly dawn when they left, and as they turned the corner at the signpost, Captain Polenski passed them on his way home.

Chapter III

It takes one green mind to recognise another
(B. O. P. Bk. 1)

Middlesex and the twins were late down for breakfast the next morning, which was hardly surprising. Stephan and Anna Polenski sat, lingering over their coffee; but the Captain could not concentrate either on his mail or the morning paper. He impatiently awaited the living proof of the extraordinary story with which his wife had greeted him on arrival home. Not that he disbelieved her. Ever since the teasings (bearable) and the official grillings (unbearable) which he had personally endured, he was beyond disbelief. He was willing to accept the evidence of his eyes and ears, especially when it was corroborated by other witnesses. After all, his co-pilot and navigator had both seen that U.F.O. on the Rio de Janiero flight, even though the decision to follow it briefly had been his alone.

He looked at his wife, calmly immersed in a massive book on *The Problem of Identification in the Adolescent.*

"Do you think we have a teenage rabbit on our hands then, Anna?" he asked with half-amused curiosity.

Mrs Polenski looked up, and considered the possibility with the concern it merited. "It's a distinct possibility," she said thoughtfully. "After the erratic behaviour of last night it has to be considered. But then, how long do rabbits live?"

"I really don't know," her husband confessed, laughing.

"I wonder if they're like dogs?" she mused. "You know, one year for them is equivalent to seven for us. You see, Middlesex may only be two chronologically, with an emotional age of fourteen."

"Have you had a chat about all this yet?" the Captain asked.

"Oh yes! We had quite a long talk yesterday. It really is most fascinating. Middlesex has no idea just what he, she, it, is."

Stefan smiled. Amateur psychologist his wife might be, but her ideas, though often startling, usually pin-pointed the root of the problem, and her solutions were based on sound common-sense. He had great faith in his wife's abilities. "Well," he said, "if anyone can straighten him… her… it… out, you will." Then he began to chuckle: "Perhaps there isn't any green rabbit really, it's just a mass-hallucination or the like?"

His wife looked shocked. "Really, Stefan, after your experience!" Then she saw that he was joking, and to his great delight she became even more serious, more intense. "No, I don't think so. The green glow, which is all that the Law observed, just doesn't fit in with that theory. No, the phenomenon is real, alright," and at that moment, as though to settle the matter, the kitchen door burst open. The twins hurled themselves at their father, but, for once, his hugs were absent minded. He was having his first glimpse of Middlesex standing in the doorway.

"Come in, and meet the Captain," said Mrs Polenski. "He has heard all about you, and is most eager to meet you."

"Good morning, Captain Polenski," Middlesex responded, walking forward, green paw extended. "I do hope I am not intruding.."

"But of course not. I'm delighted to meet you," the Captain replied, taking the proffered paw. But it was only when the soft green fur closed over his hand, that the singular nature of the guest gained reality.

"Now what would you like for breakfast?" Mrs Polenski enquired. "Eggs, bacon, sausages…?"

"Please, no," Middlesex replied quickly. "You see, I am a strict vegan."

The family looked suitably bewildered. Then Middlesex saw a carton standing on the table with the name of its contents fortunately written in capitals: MUESLI.

"I will breakfast on that, if I may, Mrs Mum," said Middlesex. "No, no, without milk, We vegans eat neither flesh nor eggs; no cheese, cream, butter or milk. The poisons they contain would dull my greenness.."

"About your greenness," said Mrs Polenski, putting the twins' breakfast on the table. "Were you, by any chance, out last night?"

Sergei began to giggle, ignoring Dasha's attempts to quieten him by an agonised *shh...* expression on her face. Then Middlesex began to giggle, and nearly choked on the Muesli.

"Alright, let's have it - all of it," said the Captain. "We have the Law's version; now let's hear yours.."

So it all had to be told: first by the twins, and then carried on by Middlesex. By the time the story ended, the violent and repeated explosions of laughter were giving them all indigestion. Slowly they subsided, wiping away the tears and gasping for breath.

"But why were P.C. Ted and P.C. Bill up there?" Dasha asked at last.

"They were checking on Sir Magnus's plane in the old hangar," her mother explained. "Apparently they go up there most nights, but I don't think they'll be too keen from now on."

"I must go in to see them, to explain and apologise," said Middlesex, suddenly serious. "And I must acquaint them with the comforting conclusion reached by G-R-I-L that, if a story of a strange green glow that haunts the place is circulated, they will find it unnecessary to patrol up there anymore. The supernatural is the ultimate deterrent."

"You're going to the Police Station?" The Captain as incredulous.

"But of course," Middlesex replied calmly. "I would not like to be responsible for two police constables going out of their lawful minds. I shall go this very morning.."

"This I must see!" exclaimed the Captain.

"We'll all go," Mrs Polenski decided. "I've some shopping to do anyway. You must tell me what you like to eat," she added to Middlesex.

"My tastes are very simple. Fruit, vegetables; in fact, anything green," Middlesex replied, "and I must introduce you all to the lettuce cornet - it's simply delicious.."

The little village of Farthingale Inferior had been the setting for many strange events during its three-thousand years of history. Romans, red-bearded Vikings and blonde Anglos had all visited it uninvited; to kill the men and mate with the women. William the Conqueror had magnanimously given it to Sir Hubert de Verte to do with as he liked - and he did! It was even rumoured that one of the Doomsday Inland Revenue men had slept in the manor house, of which only the moat, now shrunk to a duck-pond, remained. Witch hunts, wife-duckings in the duck pond and the occasional executions of petty thieves and sheep-stealers had kept the village amused all through the Middle Ages. Dwile flunkings, 'Harvest Homes' and May Day revelries had been witnessed annually by the white thatched cottages that surrounded the village green on three sides. Villagers made homeless by the enclosures had gathered there at the start of their long perilous journey to the American colonies and the local 'Dad's Army' had done its drill there in the dark days of the Second World War, marching and counter-marching round the memorial to the dead of the First, which stood in the centre of the Green. But nothing, in the long saga of sad and happy events, could match the sunny June weekend when Farthingale Inferior was adopted by a green rabbit.

The old Polenski estate car arrived in the village as the church clock in the round Norman tower was striking eleven. A few youngsters were wheeling round the Green in bored circles on their sophisticated bikes; the handful of shops were doing a brisk weekend trade and the street was littered with cars. Outside the Police house, two neat, navy Police vans were parked, one gaudy patrol car and a sleek, contented silver Rolls Royce. The Captain, swearing under his breath at the absence of a parking space, drove round the Green and parked near the duck pond. By unspoken agreement, the Polenskis loosely encircled Middlesex as they walked back across the Green. This was so successful a camouflage that only one youngster shouted something about being a month too late for the fancy-dress parade at the fair. They crossed the road successfully too, and were just turning in at the gate of the Police house when something caught Middlesex's eye, and cover was broken.

To the right of the Police house there was a large courtyard, on the far side of which sprawled the pink walls and thatched roof of the village pub, standing sideways on to the road. In the centre of the courtyard, the large inn-sign gleamed in the bright sunshine. This was the attraction Middlesex had spied the crowned head of a bearded human, tastefully painted in varying shades of green. Above the head it read "THE GREEN KING," and below "R.A.C." with "approved" in lower case letters. The latter Middlesex ignored on principle, as being unworthy of attention by a well-disciplined mind. Itself gazed up at the sign reverently, while the Polenskis hastily regrouped.

"This is truly remarkable," Middlesex murmured. "Last night, evidence of the one-time presence of a Green Rabbit on the airfield, and now a memorial to a Green Human. There must be a connection! And for that matter to be clinched by the seal of the Rabbit Aristocratic Club is truly astounding.."

"But..." the Captain began, only to immediately give up. Where could one begin with such an extraordinary individual?

Mrs Polenski searched for the point at which to attack this perfect reasoning, based on a suspect premise. The twins wondered why they had never read the sign properly before.

"I must speak to the landlord," Middlesex said. "I'm sure he will be able to give me some very valuable information," and made towards the door.

"Later, later," the Captain said, blocking the way. "They don't open till lunchtime, and ought we not to see the Police first?"

"I'm so sorry, I'd forgotten." Middlesex was full of apologies, and the little flotilla moved off to the Police house.

As the Captain rang the bell at the side door, which gave onto the official annexe, there were sounds of angry voices. P.C. Plunkett opened the door, hot and flustered, ready to do battle. Then he saw the Captain.

"Ah! Captain Polenski., do come in please. We are..." his voice trailed away. He had seen Middlesex. There was a pause, a long pause. Another face appeared, peering over his shoulder; the irate face of his Sergeant from the nearby town of Westbury. He regarded the little group; then stared in blank amazement at Middlesex.

"May we come in? We may be able to be of some assistance to you," the Captain said at last.

Animation returned to the two policemen. P.C. Bill stood back, and the whole party trooped into the tiny office. Seated on the only chair was Sir Magnus. Sir Magnus who lived at Farthingale New Hall – a charming red-brick, million-windowed Manor house that had been new when the first Elizabeth was Queen, - and who farmed the land all round WORLD'S END.

He was wearing, in deference to the heat wave, brown cavalry twill trousers, an immaculate white linen jacket and a dark-blue silk cravat. A monocle was fixed firmly over his perfectly-visioned right eye, but his silver hair, though shining and in perfect order was worn rather long, to subtly convey the message that he was, after all, a man of his times.

P.C. Ted Wimble was standing behind the diminutive counter, bristling with injured innocence. As the group spread out Middlesex was fully revealed.

Sir Magnus adjusted his monocle. "Must we be interrupted at this moment ?" he asked irritably. Then he saw the Captain and his manners improved. "Captain Polenski, good morning! I didn't notice you... this apparition in fancy dress took my eye, I'm afraid. And Mrs Polenski. I hope you are well?"

"And good morning to you, Sir Magnus," Mrs Polenski's response was uncharacteristically loud and gushing. "We are all fine, thank you, and enjoying this wonderful weather.." Though she liked what little she knew of him well enough, the clinical side of her nature rather enjoyed Sir Magnus's minor delusions of grandeur, and she always encouraged him to indulge them. "But please allow me to introduce you to our guest. Sir Magnus, this is

Middlesex. Middlesex, meet our neighbour, Sir Magnus de Verte. He lives up at Farthingale Hall and," she tried to instil caution into her tone, "he farms all the land round the old airfield and WORLD'S END."

If the message was received, Middlesex gave no sign of it, but confidently stepped forward, paw extended. "Delighted to meet you, Sir Magnus. G-R-A-S-S intimates that this is a meeting of great significance."

Years of practice, first as a minor diplomat and later as a business tycoon with world-wide interests, had conditioned Sir Magnus to accept any proffered hand with good grace, no matter what its colour or condition.

Yet, when his tanned, manicured hand sank into the living green fur, even his habitual urbanity was put to the test. "But I am afraid," Middlesex went on unperturbed, "you must be extremely annoyed at my unforgivable antics last night. I do hope that I was not responsible for too much damage. It really was inexcusable behaviour on my part, and I owe these two constables a sincere and humble apology as well."

But Sir Magnus was deaf to Middlesex's apology. His mind was on other, more exciting things than the state of his corn. With that flair and unpredictability which were the despair of his own staff, and the envy of his rivals, he concentrated now on the possibilities presented by this amazing apparition.

"Your costume is so remarkable! One would never guess that you were not an authentic rabbit - large perhaps and the wrong colour, but so life-like! Where did you obtain it from?"

"From my parents, I suspect," Middlesex replied slyly. "I can assure you that the costume is authentic, down to the last detail," and Itself turned slightly and flicked the small excuse of a tail. The twins realised that they had not even noticed it before.

"Marvellous, marvellous!" Sir Magnus experienced one of those sudden enthusiasms, which had landed him in many an odd situation in the past to explode the dull routine of life. "We must have a party - a fancy dress party, and you must let me in on your secret!"

"My secret is no secret," Middlesex replied, fixing Sir Magnus with the darkly velvet eyes, and holding his gaze until the monocle fell away from Sir Magnus's vivid blue eye. Then, almost like a chant, Middlesex intoned: "I am a Rabbit, a Green Rabbit, and a founder member of the Rabbit Aristocratic Club."

Sir Magnus sat down quietly on his chair, mesmerised by the limpid depths those brightly black eyes. "You are a Rabbit, a Green Rabbit," he repeated as though in a trance. The spell seemed to break even as he finished speaking; his tone became brisk. "But of course, you are a Green Rabbit. How stupid of me not to have recognised you straight away."

"Not to worry," said Middlesex graciously. "Now, I do like this idea of a fancy dress party. As Monday is Midsummer Eve end the weather is so perfect, could we have it on the village green? A spot of Merrie England and all that?"

It was a suggestion after Sir Magnus's own heart. "But of course. What a wonderful idea! And Midsummer Eve! Simply splendid!"

"For the whole village?" Middlesex enquired hopefully.

"For the whole village," Sir Magnus agreed. "And now, if you will all excuse me, I must get busy with the arrangements."

The Sergeant, who had been watching all this as though it was a play on a far-distant stage, suddenly came back to life. "But your complaint, Sir Magnus? Don't you want to file a... ?"

Sir Magnus waved him silent with an imperious gesture. "Don't bother me with such boring trivia, Sergeant. There's a party to be arranged - so much to think of... beer, cider... a disco... lights... refreshments. Perhaps you would help by touring round with the loud- hailer and make sure that everyone - but everyone, hears of the open invitation... and arrange the parking so that the Green isn't cluttered with cars."

The Sergeant was persistent. "But the damage to your crops?"

Middlesex joined in. "If there is any way in which I can recompense you, Sir Magnus?"

"That you have already done," Sir Magnus said warmly. "Now forget about it, please! First, I must go and see Landlord Tubble about some casks of his best brew. I shall be in touch," he added, turning to Middlesex. Then he turned to the Polenskis and bowed slightly, "Now, if you will excuse me, Captain; Mrs Polenski; children."

The grand exit, however, was disrupted by Middlesex. "If you have no objection, Sir Magnus, I will accompany you. I would like a few words with Mr Tubble. He must be a mine of information!"

"I'd be delighted," Sir Magnus said gallantly. "We'll sup a cool draught together. This place is like the hot-house at Kew."

The others watched, in silence, the little charade that was then enacted at the door as Middlesex and Sir Magnus bowed and waved each other through, and they were not surprised when the Green Rabbit took precedence! As the door closed behind the unlikely couple, the little office dissolved into a babble of talk and laughter, until the Sergeant rapped on the counter for silence.

"That would seem to be the end of this investigation," he announced in lugubrious official tone. "As Sir Magnus has generously decided not to file a complaint, and as I don't really... can't really...am at a loss to understand all that has happened here this morning, I shall declare this enquiry closed... No! Null and void! I think it might be wiser not to submit a report on it upstairs."

"Upstairs?" asked Sergei, desperately trying to follow the course of events.

"He means his superiors," his mother explained.

"I think that is a sensible decision," the Captain agreed. "So we will be on our way now."

"I think Sir Magnus is jolly nice," Dasha observed, as they made their way out of the door.

The Captain was following his family, when the Sergeant suddenly called him back. "Excuse me, Captain," he said in a low confidential whisper, "but I wonder if you could give me an assurance."

"If I can," the Captain responded co-operatively, "what is it that you want to know?"

The Sergeant cleared his throat. "Could you vouch to the fact that your guest is not an alien?"

"An alien?"

The Sergeant looked uncomfortable, but he persisted. "Yes, sir. Not of foreign origin, that is to say."

The Captain laughed. "I thought for a moment you meant a creature from outer space - a bug-eyed monster or the like!"

The Sergeant was hurt. "Oh no, sir, something far more sinister. A Commie Agent, perhaps? As we know from the papers they get up to all kinds of tricks these days, and I didn't like the effect he had on Sir Magnus."

The Captain regarded him incredulously. He smiled a gentle smile, and spoke in a gentle tone, as though to a seven year old, "But Middlesex is a Green Rabbit, Sergeant, not a red one!" and walked out through the door.

"Thank you, sir," the Sergeant said involuntarily, trying to weigh up in his own mind whether keeping silent to save face was justified, in view of any possible threat to National Security. The Sergeant, however, was of a sensitive nature, and National Security lost the contest.

CHAPTER IV
GIVE a little praise and TAKE a little credit
(B. O. P. Bk. 2)

It was still half an hour to opening time, but Landlord Tubble knew better than to argue when he saw Sir Magnus at the door. He would just have to invite him, as his guest, and the cider would be "on the house" until a suitable adjustment could be made on the quarterly account for The Hall. He did hesitate briefly, however, when he saw Sir Magnus's companion.

"Good morning, Landlord," Sir Magnus called cheerily. "I want you to meet my good friend, Middlesex. And Middlesex, meet our estimable Mr Tubble, forty years landlord of The Green King."

Under other circumstances, Mr Tubble might have proved awkward; but he had been reared in the halcyon days when "The gentry still knew best." Accordingly he shook hands, and drew two glasses of potent cider from the cask reserved for the connoisseurs of the crab-apple.

"Turning into a real scorcher today, ain't it be, Sir?" he remarked conversationally. "You must be fair roasting in that old getup, if I may say so, sir," he added, addressing Middlesex.

"My heat-regulating system is designed to cope with all extremes of temperature," Middlesex replied equably, gazing round at the untouched charm of the tap-room. The ceiling was low and beamed, from the days when the locals were heavy-shouldered but short in stature. The large, open fireplace of red Suffolk brick still had the white ashes of the last log fire of winter in it. Down the dark beams which grew unevenly in the lath and plaster walls, gleamed horse brasses which, fifty years ago, had hung proudly on the dark leather harness of Suffolk Punches.

Mr Tubble did not even bother to try to decipher Middlesex's formal speech. It was enough that the very obscurity of it marked him as one of "the gentry."

Then Middlesex smelt the cider and put down the glass. "Would you possibly have a glass of chilled cabbage water? I'm afraid that I do not touch any kind of alcohol. No offence intended, I assure you, but the greenness of my fur is of paramount importance, you see."

Mr Tubble was suitably shaken. Without thinking, to calm himself, he picked up the rejected glass and imbibed it at one gulp.

"Come, Landlord," urged Sir Magnus, "A glass of chilled cabbage water, if you please."

"I'm afraid... I've never heard of... I'm afraid we don't keep it," Mr Tubble stammered out.

"Then I trust you will do so in future ," Sir Magnus said testily. "However, the purpose of my visit is to put a sizeable amount of business your way."

Mr Tubble's expression brightened. "That's good news to me, Sir Magnus," he said happily. "What with this canned beer and all this rubbishy lager stuff from foreign parts, us pubs have been hit hard. All this drinking in the front parlour - I don't hold with it, I don't. It's not decent to my way of thinking. There's a place for everything, I always say, and pubs be the right place for drinking. 'Course, it's different for the gentry," he added as a diplomatic afterthought.

"I'm sure you're right, Tubble," Sir Magnus agreed, "But I do hope you will not disapprove of what I am going to ask you. I really shall need your help."

"You know I always do my very best for you, Sir," Mr Tubble protested. "If you say it's right and proper, that's enough for me."

They shook hands on it, and both men had the unspoken, mutual understanding that the degree of propriety was in direct relation to size of the return on the venture. They were both, after all, good business men, and respected each other for it.

"Good, good! Excellent!" Sir Magnus declared. "Now, on Monday, which is Midsummer's Eve, I am planning to throw a huge party on the Green. Everyone is to be invited; everyone that will come in costume, that is. It will be the greatest fancy-dress party that this county has ever seen!"

"And this gentleman is to be your star turn, I shouldn't wonder, Sir!" Mr Tubble shouted with a great wave of relief. Of course, it's a chap, he told himself; must be a midget though, dressed up.

"Mr Tubble, landlord of the Green King, it ill becomes you to doubt my authenticity!" Middlesex proclaimed loudly. "I am a Green Rabbit - founder member of the Rabbit Aristocratic Club. I know you must be aware of its existence, and there are many questions I would like to ask you."

The one word which commanded Mr Tubble's attention out of Middlesex's harangue, was the word 'aristocratic'.

"If I can, Sir, if I can," he mumbled dutifully.

"Good. I'm sure that we understand one another," Middlesex continued. "I applaud your reticence over the implications of the R.A.C. displayed on your inn-sign."

Mr Tubble grasped at any word he could understand. "The R.A.C. is it, Sir? Yes, we are very proud to be approved by the Royal Auto..."

"Come, come!" Middlesex interrupted in a wheedling tone. "Let us, at last, give it it's correct interpretation: The Rabbit Aristocratic Club initials, is it not?"

And, as he listened, Mr Tubble felt compelled to look into the dark velvet of the rabbit eyes; his senses seduced into a warm acceptance of this new truth.

"That's a relief," he confessed, listening in happy wonder to the words coming from his own lips. "I have had to keep the secret for so long, ever since I was a nipper, that I was fair believing the cover-up name myself."

"You've done a good job, Tubble!" Sir Magnus congratulated him.

"Now, back to the business in hand. I can rely on you to supply suitable liquid refreshments on Monday? And the bill, of course, comes to me."

"But of course, with pleasure Sir," Tubble assured him. "And I'll bring up the wooden benches and trestle tables from the cellar.

They haven't seen the light of day since this Queen's coronation, bless her."

"Capital, capital," Middlesex enthused. "And you will have a goodly supply of chilled cabbage water, won't you?" Tubble nodded. "And plenty of olives?" Middlesex added. "It is a fact that olives enhance the superb greenness of the flavour!"

"And now," Sir Magnus went on, "what about that young grandson of yours: still runs that disco-thing, does he?"

Tubble nodded. "And very successful he is with it, if I may say so, Sir Magnus. Not that I care for it myself, too much noise and caterwauling; not what I call music."

"I'm inclined to agree with you," Sir Magnus nodded. "But it is the folk music of today, and we must admit that we are the ones out of line."

"If you have him in mind for Monday, I don't know if he's booked up or not," Mr Tubble said doubtfully.

"Tell him there's fifty pounds in it for him ," Sir Magnus countered. Mr Tubble scratched his head. "I'm sure he'll do his best to oblige. 'Course, seventy would probably settle the matter, being a bit more than he usually gets, that is!"

"Sixty it is" Sir Magnus said with characteristic decisiveness, and once more the two men shook hands on it. "Fine, now I must be off, down to The Copper Kettle, and see if Mrs Gotobed and her ladies can cope with the other refreshments." He turned to Middlesex: "Are you coming, or will you stay and talk with our worthy Landlord?"

"I'll stay, if you don't mind," Middlesex replied. "But please don't hesitate to call on me if I can be of any assistance."

"Thank you so much," Sir Magnus murmured as he went out. "I'll be in touch, I do assure you."

By the time Captain Polenski arrived for a 'quick one' at the bar of the Green King, Middlesex was well established with all the regulars, and was the focus of attention. As the villagers, both native and immigrant, had drifted in for their aperitif before Saturday lunch, their reactions to the newcomer had followed a definite pattern. First, blank astonishment; then, congratulations on the excellence of the costume; finally, as they succumbed to the velvet persuasion of two rabbit eyes, acceptance of Middlesex's true condition.

In the animated conversation that Itself's questions provoked, Middlesex had already gleaned that the crowned head was commonly believed to be that of King Edmund, who was martyred by the marauding Danes in 870 A. D. at Hoxne, and was later canonized because legend had it that his severed head was guarded by a wolf. Further, from a local archaeologist came the interesting fact that a green man had often figured, in the Mystery Plays of the Middle Ages, as a symbol of life and regeneration. Then someone had added facetiously, that perhaps the yokels of past ages had dubbed the hops, from which their beer was made, "little green men." This was hotly disputed by an émigré Irishman, who said that the name obviously referred to the leprechauns. There were hoots of disparaging laughter as someone asked how leprechauns came to be in East Anglia.

Donal O'Shea waited for it to die down. "Right!" he began. "Ireland is known as the Emerald Isle, agreed?" The slightly merry company agreed, but Middlesex was listening intently. Could Ireland be his ancestral home? "And what makes it emerald?" Donal went on. "I'll tell you - Peat"

"Well? So what?" shouted one sceptic.

"Well! What have we here?" Donal shouted triumphantly.

"We have the Broads and the fens. And what are they? I ask you now - what are they? They're peat. I be telling you! Peat!"

"O. K." someone conceded. "Maybe they are, but what has that to do with the Irish?"

"It's ignorant, you are," shouted Donal, his brogue getting thicker as his excitement mounted. "And when those Fens were drained, who dug the great drainage canals, are you thinking?"

"You tell us!" a bright young thing in unisex denim shouted.

"That I will," Donal retorted hotly. "It was the navvies! And who were the navvies? They were Irishmen, I be telling you!

Dispossessed and starving so they were, by their thieving English landlords!"

"But that still doesn't tell us how the leprechauns got here," Mr Tubble protested, keeping a wary eye on his clients.

Donal downed his remaining beer and banged his glass for a refill "Have you never heard of the proverbial 'Luck of the Irish' then?" he demanded. "It's a fact, so it is, that wherever the Irish go, be it man, woman or child, their leprechauns go with them. And here, in a land of peat and open skies and rainbows, they prosper, so they do – like me!"

It was at this point that Captain Polenski interrupted. "We'd better be on our way, Middlesex," he said quietly. "The others will be wondering where we've got to."

"But of course," Middlesex agreed politely. But, before following the Captain, he addressed the company. "Thank you for a fascinating discussion, my friends. I can promise you that when G-R-I-L has had time to process all this data, I am sure we will find that your many theories fit together as pieces of a jigsaw."

"What's this G-R-I-L, Dad?" asked a Suffolk 'heavy', creaking in a studded leather jacket. "Some kind of a computer, is it then?"

"The letters stand for Green Rabbit Instant Logic," Middlesex said with dignity. "The only system of thought that will, one day, unlock the very secret of life itself."

Even the 'heavy' was somewhat taken aback by this outburst of purest blarney, and there was silence. A silence punctuated only by the swallowing of purest 'blarney' water, as Middlesex joined the Captain outside in the noonday heat.

When they got back to the car, they found that Mrs Polenski had taken off again.

"She forgot to collect the shears and sickle you took to be sharpened at Grundy's," Sergei explained, in answer to his father's question.

"Then you two had better go and help carry them," the Captain told the twins.

"Come with us, Middlesex," Dasha said, taking a green paw.

"Yes, we've hardly seen you all morning," Sergei complained, and took the other paw. And so Itself went with them.

When they got to the shop, Middlesex stopped and gazed up at the name, spelled out in faded gilt letters: G-R-U-N-D-Y.

"Now, what will that be?" Middlesex mused aloud. "Green Rabbit..."

"For Goodness sake, cut it out, Middlesex," Sergei cried.

"You've got Green Rabbit on the brain. The shop belongs to old Sam Grundy, that's all."

"Yea, maybe you're right." Middlesex felt rather relieved. Itself had the sensation of drowning in too many meaningful coincidences.

A bell tinkled as they opened the door of a shop that had changed but little in its one hundred and fifty year existence. The counter of stained teak was pitted and dusty. Row upon row of little drawers, on the wall behind it, had a sample of their contents nailed on to their fronts like variegated door handles. So brass hinges of all sizes, black door latches, glass drawer knobs, nails, screws, cold chisels, plug chains, name plates, locks, castors, domes of silence, squared and rounded cup hooks, picture hooks, curtain fittings - from brass rings to nylon brackets - created a three-dimensional collage of which any junk artist would have been proud. Mops and brooms, both ancient and modern, festooned the walls with jungle abandon; buckets, colanders, mop pails and watering cans swung suspended from the beams on giant meat-hooks.

The smell of raw metal mingled with the odour of paraffin, and a pressurized oil lamp stood displayed, sleekly white and modern, on top of the flat wooden till. Sam Grundy, whose pet hate was pre-packed ironmongery, thrilled to the feel of the crude, brittle strength of iron and the tempered tolerance of steel, as a sculptor to the feel of his stone.

Mrs Polenski was seated on the bentwood chair beside the counter, murmuring "yes" or "no" at what she hoped were the appropriate moments, as Mr Grundy explained at length why it had been necessary to put a new handle on the shears. Earnest behind his thick-lensed spectacles, with his hands in the pockets of his brown dust-coat, he could only concentrate on one thing at a time, so the entrance of a Green Rabbit went unremarked.

The twins and Middlesex wandered round, amused yet fascinated, drawing each other's attention to some fresh curiosity.

"People come here from miles away," Sergei whispered. "You can get things here that went out with the Ark. Dad says it's a little gold-mine. Mind you, old Sam knows the value of his antiques!"

"Yes," said Dasha. "When we found a pair of lovely old oil-lamps in the barn, this was the only place in the world where we could get spare parts to do them up. We use them now when there is a thunderstorm."

Sergei laughed and added, "One flash of lightning and off go the lights - and the telly! Mum says it's one of the 'joys' of country life she could do without! It's because of the overhead cables, you know."

"I rather like it ," Dasha said. "Oil lamps are cosy..."

Mrs Polenski had suddenly remembered that she wanted some tiny brass hinges for an old corner cupboard, which she and Stefan had recently picked up at an auction. Mr Grundy rummaged through his rows of drawers, and Mrs Polenski became engrossed in the specimens which he laid triumphantly on the counter. It was at this moment that Dasha became aware of the latest thing in fire-alarm systems. On a little shelf, supported by massive brackets, stood the grandfather of all brass hand-bells. Its sturdy handle was painted red, and above it a notice read: IN CASE OF FIRE - RING LOUDLY.

Giggling, she pulled Middlesex over to see it. "All mod. cons.," she whispered.

Middlesex regarded it thoughtfully for a moment, as G-R-I-D surged up within the green breast, and the green nose twitched with mischief. "I have a bad attack of G-R-I-D," Itself whispered back. "And a Green Rabbit Instant Desire is not a thing to be thwarted." A green arm reached forward and took the bell slowly and noiselessly from its perch, leaving a gleaming patch of red paint in the middle of the dust and grime of many a year. Then with the other paw on lips, Itself tip-toed out of the shop. Mrs Polenski and Mr Grundy, still engrossed in brass hinges, were blissfully unaware of the theft or of the departure of the thieves.

Once outside, still in the unabated power of G-R-I-D, Middlesex bounded across the road to the War Memorial in the middle of the Green, hotly pursued by the twins. Itself climbed the steps and began to toll the bell vigorously.

"Oyez, oyez, oyez!" Middlesex shouted in a surprisingly loud and resonant voice. "An invitation from Sir Magnus de Verte to all the citizens of Farthingale Inferior. Oyez, oyez, oyez! Gather round and listen."

The bored cyclists came quickly, pleased at this unexpected shattering of the mid-day doldrums, and waited expectantly. Middlesex swung the bell harder but in a strict tempo of 'quick, quick, slow'. The cry was repeated again with greater force, and shoppers about to return to their homes or cars walked over to see what was happening. Customers leaving the Green King saw, called out to others still in the bar, and hurried over to see the fun. The ever-watchful eyes of the surrounding houses and cottages somehow managed to communicate to those already at table or washing-up the growing excitement on the Green, and they forgot everything and hurried out to join the swelling crowd.

"Oyez, oyez, oyez!" Middlesex kept on repeating, until the size of the audience was deemed satisfactory. Then the news was proclaimed with all the verve and drama of the finest town crier: "An invitation from Sir Magnus de Verte to all who live within the confines of the parish of Farthingale Inferior! A fancy dress revelry will be held here, on the ancient Green, on Midsummer Eve, Monday the twenty-third day of June, and will continue into the early hours of Midsummer Day. Oyez oyez, oyez! Liquid refreshments by Mr Tubble, worthy landlord of The Green King; gastronomical delicacies by Mrs Gotobed of The Copper Kettle. Music will be provided by the electronic wizardry of Young Tubble's disco. Oyez, oyez, oyez! Admission by costume only."

Middlesex was getting quite carried away by the power of the orator, and went on: "Grand parade and prizes in many categories for the best costume. After dark, there will be a great display of fireworks. Don't miss the event of the year - of the decade - of the century! The revelries will commence at seven of the clock."

The twins watched and listened in helpless astonishment. Then they saw their father edging nervously through the crowd.

"Middlesex, please! Stop it" he pleaded when he was close enough. "Middlesex, you've said enough."

Itself beamed down benevolently at the Captain. "I have finished," Middlesex replied with an enormous sense of fulfilment. "I suppose I had better return the bell now," and began to walk back to Mr Grundy's shop. The crowd, talking excitedly among itself, made way. Some of the men slapped Middlesex admiringly on the back.

"Well done, old chap!"

"First rate town crier."

"Bit early with the old costume, aren't you?"

At the entrance to the shop, Middlesex turned round and gave a final demonstration of campanological prowess with three mighty swings of the hell. The resounding notes broke Mr Grundy's concentration on brass hinges and, after a momentary pause, he dashed to the telephone in his office at the back of the shop.

"Fire! Police! Ambulance!" he shouted at the operator on Emergency Services. "Grundy's shop, High Street, Farthingale Inferior. Quickly! Come quickly!" and he slammed the hand-piece down.

For over thirty years he had rehearsed that speech every Monday morning before opening, and now he experienced a wave of intense satisfaction at his word-perfect performance.

He ran back into the shop. "Who rang the bell?" he shouted.

"I'm afraid I did," Middlesex owned up guiltily, having just replaced the bell on the shelf.

Mr Grundy, however, was in such a state of excitement that he noticed neither the greenness nor the rabbitiness of the speaker.

"Well done! Well done!" he cried. "Now everybody out - quickly," and he half threw the astonished Polenskis and Middlesex out onto the pavement.

A moment later P.C. Bill arrived, breathless after his hundred yard sprint up the street. "Where's the fire then, Mr Grundy?" he shouted.

Mr Grundy suddenly realised that he had not the slightest idea, and he looked round the shop with growing bewilderment.

"Must be in the basement," he cried with a flash of inspiration, and the two men went crashing down the steps at the back of the shop.

Out on the pavement, Sergei pulled Middlesex to one side. "Now you've gone and done it!" he whispered reproachfully. "There'll be one big heap row now."

"But it was so eminently worth it," Middlesex retorted, still unabashed, and not yet quite free of the spell of G-R-I-D. "And don't worry, I've got a guardian leprechaun - the luck of the Irish and all that!"

"I haven't a clue what you're talking about," Sergei said impatiently. "And look out! Here comes Dad!"

The Captain went straight to his wife. "Are you alright, Anna?" he asked anxiously.

"Yes, of course," Mrs Polenski replied. "Apparently Middlesex smelt or saw something, and rang the alarm bell."

"Is that so?" the Captain said suspiciously. He turned to the twins: "And what do you two know about all this?"

Their confusion, fortunately, was lost in the excitement as the local fire tender arrived. The men were in various stages of undress, struggling with helmets and jacket buttons and belts. Some of them had even run straight from the performance on the Green to the fire station. They jumped down from the tender, axes at the ready, and charged into Mr Grundy's shop like a tribe of Red Indiana on the warpath. At that moment Mr Grundy emerged from the cellar.

"Where's the fire then?" they cried. "Must we get the thatch off?"

"No, no," Mr Grundy shouted in alarm. "Nothing like that. In fact, there seems to have been a... a mistake!"

P.C. Bill appeared. "No sign of a fire down there," he said sharply. "Who did you say gave the alarm, Mr Grundy?"

"It was a gentleman... no, I tell a lie. It was a... I don't know who it was... really," and his voice trailed away, as his returning memory made the most ridiculous suggestion.

The firemen, deflated by this anti-climax, began to look angry. P.C. Bill, however, kept his cool, using those deductive powers of reasoning which all good policemen possess, and asked suspiciously: "Was it a green and furry individual, of short height and... and like this?" and he pointed to Middlesex who had just come in through the door.

Before the confused Mr Grundy could make any comment, Middlesex took command of the situation. "Capital, Capital!" The words were wrapped in the aura of warmest congratulation. "By my reckoning the Police were here within four minutes of the call going out, and the fire tender in eight. A truly magnificent performance by all concerned!"

Involuntarily, a warm glow of achievement spread through the broad chests of P.C. Bill and the six men of the Farthingale part-time Fire Brigade, although P.C. Bill managed to continue the struggle against the illogicality of the situation.

"So it was you?" he said, with as much outraged authority as he could summon.

"Yes, indeed, it was I!" Middlesex confirmed proudly. "And I feel that a letter to the local press, commending the high state of efficiency of all concerned, is a top priority," Itself went on magnanimously. "From Mr Grundy who reacted so promptly and with such precision, to the Ambulance crew who have just arrived, I perceive. Ten minutes in all! Capital, Capital!"

In the stunned silence which followed this peroration, the Captain intervened. "If you're quite satisfied, Constable," he said quickly, "I'll take Middlesex home now."

P.C. Bill nodded, a nod compounded of resignation and bewilderment; but that was enough for the Captain. Hastily he shepherded his wife, the twins and, most firmly of all, Middlesex, through the little crowd outside the door, and back into the car. The village, he decided, would have to sort it out for themselves.

Middlesex leant back in the car and beamed contentedly. "A capital morning! I feel I've known this village all my life. You are all such N-I-C-E people!"

Usually, the Captain liked to amble along the narrow lanes back to WORLD'S END, but today his foot went down and the journey resembled a pitch-back ride.

"It may be that Middlesex has problems," he said at last to his wife in a low voice. "But on present reckoning, I would say Itself is a past master at creating them."

Mrs Polenski laughed: "But you must admit, Stefan, that this has been the most entertaining morning we've ever spent in the village."

And slowly the Captain's sense of the absurd reasserted itself, for it was never very far below the surface. By the time they turned in at the white barred gate, only Sergei was in sober mood. He still could not quite work out how Middlesex managed to get away with such outrageous behaviour and, although he did not like to admit it even to himself, he knew that he was green - with envy!

CHAPTER V

To be in the right place, at the right time, is a necessary green act.
(B. O. P. Bk. 2)

During the preparation of lunch, at which all lent a hand, everyone told everyone else their morning's adventures. Even Mrs Polenski found a sympathetic listener in Middlesex, for her grumbles about the price of greengroceries and the state of the economy. Middlesex kept his promise, and concocted five lettuce cornets out of rolled crinkly lettuce leaves filled with chopped spring onion and watercress, liberally sprinkled with French dressing and topped by a radish rosette. They were declared delicious by the Polenskis and as they ate, Middlesex recounted the discussions in The Green King.

"All seems disconnected and contradictory to me," the Captain said, when all had been told.

"I agree, it does," Middlesex conceded. "However, after lunch I shall retire and subject it to G-R-I-L."

"G-R-I-L?" , the Captain queried.

"Green Rabbit Instant Logic," Dasha translated, laughing. "It has an answer for everything!"

"As was demonstrated this morning," Middlesex was smug.

"How do you mean?" , Sergei demanded eagerly.

"Well now, you see," Middlesex started in confidential tones, "in that little fracas over the fire alarm; when I realized that I had acted a trifle impulsively, G-R-I-L advised me to enhance the self-esteem of those who felt I bad offended. By stating no more than the truth, that they had all reacted admirably, I increased their tolerance of my innocent prank."

"What you mean," Sergei laughed, a little cynically, "is that flattery will get you anywhere, and out of any scrape."

Middlesex was offended. "No, I do not mean that: flattery is insincere and, even if true, overstates the case. But my admiration for P.C. Bill, the brave firemen and the ambulance crew is one hundred per cent genuine. Inadvertently, I gave them an opportunity to demonstrate their prowess and, I am sure, they all feel much improved by the exercise."

In point of fact, P.C. Bill, the firemen and the ambulance crew, were downing pints of sanity in The Green King, and mutually agreeing to erase the whole incident from their memories. Unfortunately they had forgotten Middlesex's promise - or was it threat? - to write to the local press. It was doubly unfortunate, in this case, that Middlesex always honoured a promise.

The afternoon passed peacefully at WORLD'S END. Middlesex wrote the letter in finest capitals, and then wandered off through the corn to find a suitable retreat for an uninterrupted session of G-R-I-L. Beyond the hangars there was a sheltered hollow, carpeted by daisy, speedwell and buttercup, and there Middlesex lay down on the springy turf. For three hours Itself slept, while G-R-I-L reduced the welter of information into some kind of order. When the internal clock struck tea-time, Middlesex awoke refreshed and carefree, secure in the conviction that it was all beginning to make sense - Green Rabbit Sense!

The twins spent the afternoon up in one of the attics, trying to assemble costumes for the Midsummer romp. Dasha decided that she would be a bunny girl, slightly modified, in the style of the Playboy Clubs, of which she had found a picture in a magazine. For a long time Sergei was uninspired until he came across a tatty 'Topper' at the bottom of the wardrobe.

"That's it," he said. "The Mad March Hare - and let's see what our mad June Rabbit makes of that!"

As the family re-assembled for their evening meal, Mrs Polenski was taken unawares when a sleek Rolls Royce purred up to the gate and stopped.

"Stefan," she called her husband urgently, "Sir Magnus is paying us a call; what can he possibly want?"

Her husband put down the white wine he was decanting and joined her. "I don't really want to hazard a guess," he said warily.

Sir Magnus apologised long and profusely for his unheralded visit, but said he had heard a rather disquieting rumour about Middlesex.

"Here we go," the Captain whispered despairingly to his wife, as he went to fetch Middlesex. But when Green Rabbit and the Bart saw each other, the Polenskis were hard-pressed not to laugh out loud at the reunion: a re-union that smacked of a life-long friendship renewing itself after years of enforced separation!

The formalities over, Sir Magnus turned to the twins. "Have you decided on your costumes yet?" he asked benevolently.

"Yes, we have," Sergei answered, feeling a little out of his depth. "Haven't we Dasha?"

"Yes, but they're a secret," she replied, discretion having suddenly struck her. It would be as well, she had just realized, if her father was left in blissful ignorance of her choice until the hour of the party.

"That's fine! Secrets are always exciting," Sir Magnus smiled. "And I want Monday to be a day, and a night, that will be remembered for many a long year to come!"

"I think you can rest assured, Sir Magnus, that it most surely will be a memorable occasion!" the Captain remarked dryly.

"But," said Sir Magnus turning to Middlesex, "what is this I hear, my friend. You promised 'em fireworks. Could be most awkward at this time of year, and at such short notice, don't you know!"

"I'm so sorry!" Middlesex was instantly contrite. "I'm afraid I got a bit carried away. Still, I can always make some!"

"Over my dead body!" the Captain cried unceremoniously.

There was a brief, awkward silence until Sergei had a minor brain-wave. "I wonder," he said, "what happened to all those that the Parish Council bought last year? Don't you remember, Mum, it just rained and rained right through November, and we never had them?"

"Yes, you're right, Sergei," his mother agreed. "I think it was finally decided to keep them for next year."

"In that case, the problem is solved," Sir Magnus said confidently. "I know old Perkins very well. It'll just take a small bonus to cover the inflationary trend to persuade him to sell them, I'm sure!"

"That is worthy of G-R-I-L," Middlesex said admiringly.

"Yes, my friend," Sir Magnus went on, "when a thing is meant to be, all problems can be resolved. At least, that is the philosophy by which I live - very successfully, if I may be so immodest."

"G-R-I-L, G-R-A-S-S and I, salute you," Middlesex was jubilant. "You have a philosophy worthy of your name."

"My name?" Sir Magnus was mystified.

"De Verte!" Middlesex cried. "De Verte - of The Green! If there are truly such monstrosities as 'blue-blooded' humans you are certainly not of their number. No, you belong to the Green Aristocrats of creation, like me - and my good friends here."

"How fascinating! What an original mind you have, old friend. But do go on." Sir Magnus was entranced, for he had never really recovered from a long-ago Biology lesson where he had first learned that blue-blood was impure blood!

"You'll have to excuse me, Sir Magnus," Mrs Polenski broke in suddenly. "The dinner is spoiling."

Sir Magnus sniffed appreciatively. "It smells most appetizing, Mrs Polenski."

Mrs Polenski looked across at her husband and winked. He smiled and nodded his head.

"Would you care to join us, Sir Magnus?" she asked.

Sir Magnus beamed. At home, his only dinner companion would be himself, for the Lady Beatrice, his wife, was out in the Australian Bush deciphering Aborigine totem poles for the Royal Geographical Society.

"I'd be delighted, absolutely delighted!" he purred "It is kind of you!"

With all the innocence of one not used to servants, Dasha posed the next awkward question. "What about your chauffeur?" she asked.

"Oh, don't worry about Danvers," Sir Magnus replied airily. "He's used to waiting. That's what he's paid for!"

A wicked grin spread across Anna Polenski's attractive face. "But it's so unnecessary," she protested, going towards the door. "He will be so bored - and hungry too. There's plenty in the pot for us all."

Sir Magnus accepted defeat with a suitable spirit of adventure.

It would be, at least, a novel experience to sit down at the dinner table with his chauffeur. At best, it might prove enlightening.

"Capital," Middlesex was delighted. "You have proved yourself a true 'greener', Sir Magnus. Attention to the false distinctions of class are the mark of the inferior 'blue-blooders'. We are the true aristocrats, who have no need of segregation to prove our worth!"

"Quite, quite," Sir Magnus agreed. "You have a most original mind - most original."

During the early part of dinner, the conversation was limited mainly to "More cabbage, Middlesex?" and "Have you had the gravy, dear?" or "Pass the mint sauce, Dasha." But by the time the strawberry cheesecake had been served, it gathered momentum.

Sir Magnus passed on the cream jug and asked: "Was Tubble of any help to you, Middlesex? He's always eager to please, but often gets the wrong end of the stick, poor chap."

"He did his best," Middlesex replied generously. "However, as the bar filled up, some very interesting theories were tossed about."

"They all sounded to pretty well cancel each other out" the Captain volunteered. "What does your... your..."

"Green Rabbit Instant Logic," Sergei filled in.

"Thank you, Sergei. Your G-R-I-L make of it, then?"

"But what is it, precisely, that you want to know?" Sir Magnus broke in ingenuously, before Middlesex could reply to the Captain.

"Everything, just everything," Middlesex answered disarmingly. "You see, Sir Magnus, I know nothing of myself which is not of the present. I know nothing of my origin, age, parentage, sex even. Only that I am alive and unique - and founder member of R.A.C."

Suddenly Danvers, steadily gaining in confidence at the side of Mrs Polenski, who had been experimenting at the inflation of his ego, found his voice. "What about ley lines then?" he asked inconsequentially. "I bet someone as sensitive as you, sir, responds to them."

Sir Magnus put his monocle firmly into position and regarded his chauffeur with surprise. "Ley lines, Danvers? What in carnation are ley lines?"

Justifiable pride lit up Mrs Polenski's eyes. "Ley lines, Sir Magnus," she said, with the merest trace of intellectual superiority, "Ley lines are lines of magnetic force which can be scientifically demonstrated. Recent research into ancient stone edifices, from the Mediterranean to the Outer Hebrides, seem to indicate that the peoples of pre-history had an awareness that sadly we have lost."

"And one actually passes through Farthingale," Danvers went on, encouraged by Mrs Polenski's support. "It ends up at Bury St. Edmunds."

"Very interesting," Middlesex proclaimed loudly. "I have certainly been aware on my travels that I seem, at various times, to have been drawn in a certain direction. And most certainly, I had a compelling sense of direction which led me to the signpost to BY ROAD and into your delightful company."

"Perhaps it's your metal R.A.C. Medallion," Sergei said jokingly, "acting as a receiver or something?"

But Middlesex was serious. "Drawing me to the very place where Green Rabbits have been known and respected for centuries. G-R-I-L accepts the theory without reservation. It fits in with all the present known facts. Thank you, Mr Danvers; thank you, Sergei!"

Sir Magnus was lost - this was hardly his line of country. "Something there for Beatrice to work on when she gets home" he said, with a hint of petulance.

"Shall we take our coffee into the lounge?", the Captain suggested tactfully. "And then, Middlesex, you can fill us in about G-R-I-L's final conclusions on the matter."

"If you'll forgive me, sir," Danvers was getting braver by the minute, "conclusions, if final, are counter-productive."

"You're a very wise man," Middlesex applauded. "But I will enlighten you on the open-ended progress achieved by G-R-I-L."

But it was not to be! As they all settled down, Sir Magnus suddenly remembered that his very special cigars were still in the car. "I really must honour your splendid meal by smoking one," he told his hostess. "And perhaps you would care to join me, Captain? They're a very fine blend."

Danvers stood up to go and fetch them, but he was forestalled by Middlesex. "Allow me: I could do with a whiff of night air," and beckoning the twins to follow, disappeared through the door. Once outside, restraint gone, the three of them raced down the path and clambered over the three-barred gate. Middlesex opened the driver's door reverently, and sniffed the expensive aroma of the car appreciatively. Unfortunately, the twins were not yet wise enough to recognise the warning signs of an impending attack of G-R-I-D.

"Climb in," the twins were urged, and the rear door swung open. "Climb in and get the feel of Royalty!"

They did not need to be told a second time, and hopped into the back without a single qualm. After a moments grace, they began to experiment with the gadgetry. They tried out the intercom with the driver; pressed buttons and windows went up and down, cigar lighters popped up glowing dully; a radio blared out and a tape-recorder whirred discreetly. Then the panel at the bottom of the screen between the front and the rear of the car, folded back to reveal bottles of brandy, scotch and gin with attendant glasses, olives and cocktail cherries.

Next they picked up the telephone receiver and dialled an imaginary number which, fortunately, gave them the "unobtainable" bleeps. They were so engrossed that they did not hear the engine spring, cat-purring smooth, to life. It was only when Middlesex fumbled the reverse lever on the automatic controls, that they realised they were in motion.

"Stinging rattlesnakes!" Sergei roared over the intercom, "What do you think you're doing?"

Middlesex completed a three-point turn with style, and proceeded up the lane to the BY ROAD signpost before speaking sedately back through the intercom. "Right or left, Sir? Madam?"

"Stop it," Dasha shouted back. "Middlesex, stop it!"

"Don't worry, I am an excellent driver, Madam," came the obsequious reply. "I shall turn right in the absence of further instructions."

Dasha and Sergei looked at each other helplessly. "He's mad!" asserted Sergei.

"Not too mad to be really able to drive, I hope," said Dasha nervously.

She need not have worried. Middlesex drove with great panache along the darkening country roads at an average of fifty miles an hour; the brilliant headlights illumining the sleeping hedgerows in the dusky June night. The car braked smoothly but sharply a number of times as Middlesex gave precedence to a mouse crossing the road; or to let a hare, at first dazzled by the lights and then swearing at them, gain the security of a field of corn. At each emergency stop, a polite *Oops, sorry about that* drifted back through the intercom, to be followed by crazy hoots of laughter and loud snatches of song.

The twins relaxed slowly in this warm torrent of absurd noise, until they too joined in the singing and roared with laughter at each *Oops, sorry about that*. Middlesex began to twiddle knobs and press buttons and switches. Windscreen wipers swung in low arcs; water squirted up; windows played a 'now you see me, now you don't' game; pop music came and went; fog lights reinforced the headlights, and air was blown at hurricane force round the car.

"Tonight I am omnipotent," Middlesex shouted. "All this power at my finger-tips. I am the irresistible force and... oops, what's this then?" The car braked so sharply that Dasha and Sergei landed on the floor.

Middlesex sprang out of the Rolls, and ran to a bundle lying not two yards from the front wheel of the car. Only the strength of the power headlights had enabled Middlesex to stop before the wheels made contact. The bundle groaned. With tender paws, Middlesex turned the bundle over. It was P.C. Ted, and his bike was lying a few feet away under a tree at the road's edge.

Dasha and Sergei were at Middlesex's side. "What's happened?" Dasha asked anxiously. "Did you hit him?"

"No, of course we didn't," Sergei said impatiently. "He'd have been squashed flat if we had hit him, silly!"

"No, I didn't hit him," Middlesex repeated. "I don't know what has happened, but I do know that he is badly hurt. Help me to get him onto the back seat, and we'll take him to the hospital."

Somehow, they manhandled the thirteen stone of unconscious Law into the oar, and covered him with a rug. Then Sergei remembered the brandy. Slowly, P.C. Ted recovered his wits.

"It's my leg," he groaned, "it must be broken."

"Whatever happened?" Dasha was solicitous.

"I don't really know," confessed P.C. Ted. "All I remember is some joker coming towards me with his headlights full on. I was dazzled and I think I waved at him. Then I hit something... and that's the lot."

"You rode into a tree," Middlesex said. "And that joker must be the one that went swinging round the corner at the crossroads back there."

And so, ten minutes later Sir Magnus's Rolls screeched up to the Casualty Department of Westbury General Hospital. Sergei and Dasha explained as best they could to the Sister what had happened, as two stretcher bearers carried P.C. Ted inside. To the twins' relief, Middlesex stayed in the car and fiddled with the radio. They escaped as soon as they could, but not before a Patrol car, bringing the Sergeant to the hospital, turned in at the drive. It passed the Rolls halfway down. The Sergeant watched in incredulously. Only fifteen minutes earlier it had been reported stolen.

"Follow that car!" he yelled unreasonably at his driver. So precious minutes were lost as they were forced to follow the narrow drive up to the little roundabout at the front of Casualty, before they could go roaring down it again, in the hope of catching up with the Rolls.

Dasha was the first to notice that a Police car seemed to be following them, with all lights flashing. "Middlesex, stop!" she called. "The police are signalling us to stop."

That, of course, was a challenge that Middlesex could not resist.

This time Middlesex broke all records, managing, nevertheless, thanks to the instantaneous obedience of the powerful engine to the merest pressure of a foot - even a green furry one - to give right of way to other, slower nocturnal users of the road. The Rolls drew up outside WORLD'S END all of seven seconds before the Police car. They found the Captain and his wife, Sir Magnus and Danvers already out at the gate.

"Where, in the name of all that is holy, have you been?" the Captain demanded sternly, when he saw who was in the car. "We had mistakenly concluded, it would seem, that you had gone after the thieves, not that you were the thieves."

"No, Dad, listen please!" Dasha pleaded. "We've just taken P.C. Ted to hospital. He was unconscious and his leg was broken and..."

Eventually the whole story was pieced together. The Sergeant listened to it poker-aced.

"Have you a licence?" he demanded of Middlesex, when the saga was finished.

"No, Sergeant."

"Then you realize that you were committing a serious offence?"

"No, Sergeant! I know of no legislation which forbids a Green Rabbit to drive without a licence," Middlesex argued reasonably.

Wearily, the Sergeant changed tack. "Nevertheless, you have taken a vehicle without the owner's prior knowledge and consent?"

"Yes, I must admit to that," Middlesex confessed with disarming candour. "But I am sure that Sir Magnus will give it, retrospectively, when he learns that I was only complying with an insistent demand from G-R-A-S-S."

"Would you be so good as to explain?" the Sergeant said, even more wearily.

"My Green Rabbit Automatic Sixth Sense insisted that I should be on that road, at that very moment, in a suitable vehicle to render assistance to one of your men," Middlesex said smoothly; Sergei silently awarded him full marks for ingenuity.

"My dear friend, I understand perfectly," Sir Magnus purred. "There is really no need for all this melodrama, Sergeant. My car is safe; your man is safe, and I have had a most enjoyable evening with these dear people. So please, I beg of you, let us leave it that way."

"Very well," the Sergeant admitted defeat in face of overwhelming odds. "If you are satisfied, Sir Magnus, we will let the matter rest there." He went back to the Police car and departed. P.C. Wimble would have to be cautioned to be silent on the matter.

"There's only one thing, dear friend," Sir Magnus complained gently as they walked back to the cottage, "I do wish you'd popped in with the cigars before you went off on this G-R-A-S-S thing."

"I'm so sorry," Middlesex replied with genuine remorse. "And may I say, Sir Magnus, your greenness glows brighter by the hour."

CHAPTER VI

Revelation is a matter for the light and shade of perspective
(B. O. P. Bk. 3)

By approximately three-thirty on Saturday afternoon, everyone in the Parish of Farthingale Inferior knew of the forthcoming festivities. Outlying farms and homes were informed by the bush telegraph long before the Police van did its stuff with the loud-speaker equipment. Even the 'travelling folk', temporarily parked in a disused gravel pit to work at the local fruit-picking, got wind of it. As Sir Magnus was as renowned for his generosity as he was for his millions, the villagers, both native and foreign, instantly offered their help.

All through the rest of Saturday and through the golden hours of Sunday they worked. Fairy lights were festooned through the trees, and bunting that dated from Mafeking to the last Church fete was dug out of chests or from the backs of top shelves, in shed or attic. Perkins, the Parish Clerk, not only sold his hoarded fireworks to Sir Magnus at cost price plus seventy per cent inflation weighting, he also offered to rig up a display, as he did for the village bonfire every November the fifth.

The bowling alley, roll-a-penny boards, dart boards, hoop-la and other sideshow paraphernalia, owned by the locals and brought out faithfully for the Church fete every year, duly made their appearance. The Farthingale Arts group rang the Hall, offering to put on a floor show of Morris dancing; the Youth Club offered a judo display; and some 'bright young things' from the new estate for young reps and junior executives offered a comic strip-tease. To them all, Sir Magnus's secretary was instructed to say that it was their party; that the Green was big enough for them to find their own corner, and to do their own thing.

So the whole complex took shape, with all parties content, and Sir Magnus's wallet lighter by a mere five hundred pounds. The Captain and his wife lent a hand, but managed to persuade Middlesex to stay home with the twins, on the pretext of helping them with their costumes. And so the day passed peacefully enough, through the hot noon hours on the village green into the calm tranquillity of a June evening. One by two, their preparations complete, folk drifted into The Green King to find that all drinks that evening were "on the house," meaning of course, Sir Magnus' quarterly account.

The twins and Middlesex, too, had a peaceful and lazy day. The twins concocted masterpieces for their lunch from ice-cream, nuts, fruits and chocolate sauce, topped with maraschino cherries filched from the drink cupboard. Middlesex found amusement in experimenting with variations on the theme of a lettuce cornet, and the gastronomical delights were slowly imbibed under the horse chestnut tree in one corner of the garden.

"Don't you really know how old you are?" Dasha asked idly, savouring a mouthful of her sundae. "Sometimes you seem like us - you know, about twelve years old - and then with the grown-ups, you seem all grown-up! I find it confusing."

"Which confuses me too," Middlesex confessed. "Once when I stayed briefly with a nuclear physicist and his family, he said I was of no place and no time; and that, anyway, all time was co-existent."

"But that makes you sound like a ghost," Sergei objected. "And you eat too much to be a spirit."

"Precisely!" Middlesex agreed, attacking another lettuce cornet. "Naturally, I am curious, but G-R-I-L advises me to be content with the sure knowledge that I am as old as I am. And for the moment that must suffice." A suppressed giggle sent a piece of cucumber down the wrong way, and Sergei had to thump a very substantial green back to prevent a Green Rabbit from choking. When Itself had recovered, Dasha and Sergei demanded to know the joke.

"I was just remembering," Middlesex laughed, "that before I left, I rewired his electric alarm clock. I've often wondered how the Prof. coped with time going backward!"

Whereupon they nearly all choked to death. As the laughter subsided, Sergei said: "O.K. then, you are as old as you are, but what about your parents, and where you come from?"

"Again I draw a blank," Middlesex admitted, delicately licking a tomato-smeared paw. "Prior to the state when I achieved speech and ordered, logical thought, I can remember nothing. And by then, I was already embarked on The Quest!"

"But surely you must be able to remember something," Dasha persisted. Middlesex shook a head with ears limp in the noon-day heat. "No! Just think - if you had been abandoned before the age of three, say, and there was no one who could tell you anything about yourself, would you know who you were, or where you had come from?"

Dasha was all sympathy. "How terrible! How did you survive?"

"As far back as I can remember, I have been in full control of my faculties - and my destiny," Middlesex boasted.

"There you go again!" Sergei shouted, "back on your high falutin' horse again."

Middlesex was offended, and bit viciously on lettuce cornet.

"Oh don't take umbrage, as the man said, Middlesex," laughed Dasha. "He's only having you on."

"If G-R-I-L has endowed me with a sense of dignity and purpose, which you find objectionable, then I'm sorry. But that's the way I am," Middlesex said miserably.

"And that's the way we like you!" Sergei shouted, ashamed of his teasing. "Come on, let's go and get some iced orange squash."

"And I second the motion," Dasha added, having just learned the basic rules of debate at school. "Carried unanimously."

After their leisurely dinner that evening, the Polenskis received an unexpected phone call. It was Sir Magnus suggesting, that as it was such a splendid evening, they should all take - as he put it - a toddle round in his mini-airbus. The Captain declined on the grounds that, for him, it would be something of a busman's holiday. Mrs Polenski too, excused herself pleading that she had not finished their costumes and that, in any case, as Stefan had to report back for duty on Tuesday, she had a lot to do. So it was, that when Danvers arrived in the Rolls to pick them up, it was only the twins and Middlesex who went off on the great jaunt.

This time they drove up to the hangar in style. The Jetstream Executive airbus was already out on the runway, and it only remained for Danvers to exchange his chauffeur's cap for a pilot's.

"Right, all aboard!" Sir Magnus called with youthful excitement. "Now," he began as they settled into their luxurious seats and fastened safety-belts, "I thought we might circle the immediate area for a while before flying on to London. We should arrive at lighting-up time, and witness that truly magical hour when the dross of the metropolis is transformed into a pool of scattered jewels that would shame Aladdin's cave itself." His audience listened spell-bound. "Then out to sea at Tilbury to watch the shipping, and back home over the coastal towns as far as Yarmouth. They, too, are quite enchanting at this time of year with their tiaras of promenade lights. Does that sound a reasonable itinerary to you?"

"Not reasonable," Middlesex purred, "but a flight of purest imagination. It will be a unique experience as well as my initiation"

The plane taxied forward and rose smoothly up through the still, scented air. Soon Suffolk was revealed to their eyes; a vast patchwork, embracing every nuance of green known or imagined. And in field and hedgerow, finger-flicked rivulets of crimson glory blossomed where spray had missed the frail Flander's poppy. Ribbons of roads, sprinkled with toy cars, snaked through the fields and woods, pendants of model villages hanging from them in crazy array. Danvers flew in great loops, crossing and criss-crossing the area around Farthingale Inferior, and dived low once in salute over WORLD'S END. The twins, in great excitement, moved from window to window, picking out landmarks, and occasionally arguing about what was where. They had flown a few times in the great Jets that their father piloted, at heights which reduced the living world to the configurations on a map. Yet here, in a small plane elevated above, but still in contact with, the small realities, they felt as if they were astride the mobile peak of some Mount Everest. They felt they had but to stretch out a hand to possess the whole world.

Middlesex sat by the window, mesmerized by the blue and green panorama of land and sky. The sun was low, and the horizon to the west rosily proclaimed the end of one sun-drenched day and promised another.

It was Dasha, on her perambulations from window to window, who noticed it first.

"Hey!" she called "There seems to be some kind of a... a picture in the corn," and she pointed to a great complex of fields lying over to the east of Farthingale. The others hurried over to her side of the plane. The low slanting rays of the setting sun were endowing each blade of corn with a long shadow, and corporately lending depth and perspective to the crops.

"Yes, I can see some of it," Sergei shouted in great excitement. "There's a large rounded body, and an arm!"

"I can see a leg," Dasha shouted. "But it's rather fat."

"Circle and fly past again," Sir Magnus called to Danvers. "slow as you can," and he let the monocle fall from his eye so that he could see more clearly.

They came back in a slow sweep, and all of them saw the full outline at one and the same moment.

"It's a rabbit! A Green Rabbit!" Sergei shouted. "Look! There are the ears - and the legs are fat because they're not legs at all – they're haunches. Middlesex, it's a Green Rabbit!"

Middlesex was stunned. "Yes, yes, I can see it?" The words were mumbled and vague. "It's unbelievable... unbelievable!"

"Believable or not, dear friend, it's there," Sir Magnus stated categorically. "Round again, Danvers. Slow now."

Again the little plane circled. The rabbit's head was mostly in a field of grey-green oats; half the body the yellow-green of ripening wheat, and the other part and one leg the dark, dreary green of sugar beet. The right hind leg was etched in red-sheened barley, and the right arm decked in a white-and-green speckled field of beans.

They flew over it yet again, but by now the sun was on the horizon, and the vision was fading. Middlesex turned to Sir Magnus with great solemnity. "Sir Magnus de Verte! G-R-I-L thanks you; G-R-A-S-S thanks you; R.A.C. in the person of its founder member thanks you, and I thank you! This night shall come to be remembered as the night when the Green Rabbit reassumed its rightful position in the affairs of the world."

"Very kind of you, dear friend," Sir Magnus responded with a small bow, and replaced his monocle. "Now shall we continue to London? Contrast being the essence of appreciation and all that."

"But what was it?" Dasha asked, as Danvers set course for the flight path reserved for private planes flying into or over the Capital.

"A mirage or something of the kind," Sir Magnus said lightly, spoilt by the myriad extra-ordinary sights he had seen on his meanderings over the face of the globe. "Mass hallucination and all that. Jolly interesting though."

There was a discreet cough, then Danvers spoke up. "Excuse me, Sir Magnus, but I beg to differ. It is a well-documented phenomena in archaeological research that ancient earthworks, often spread over many acres, and constructed by the peoples of prehistory, are still visible from the air; especially when the sun is at a suitable angle."

"I know what you mean," Dasha said, as Sir Magnus seemed at a loss for words. "We saw all about it on the telly. Don't you remember, Sergei?"

"Oh yes," Sergei recalled. "Wasn't it some place in Somerset that we saw?"

"Glastonbury," Danvers offered. "There, it is a magic circle of the signs of the Zodiac, with the Holy Grail at the centre."

"You are remarkably well informed" commented a chastened Sir Magnus.

"As you are aware, Sir, I have a great deal of time for reading in my job, during the long waits when you are in conference *et cetera*. I hope, one day, to be able to take an Open University course."

"A splendid ambition, Danvers," Sir Magnus congratulated him. Sir Magnus believed in self-improvement. "What is holding you back?"

Danvers shifted in his seat uneasily, but knew that this was an opportunity that might never present itself again. "The fees, Sir Magnus, just the fees."

Sir Magnus waved an impatient hand. "There's no need for any difficulty there, Danvers. We must look into the matter. Make a memo. and remind me about it, please."

It was not pure altruism on Sir Magnus's part, for his alert business mind had instantly registered that the tedious journeys, which he had to endure so frequently in the course of his duties as 'Chairman' of that and 'Managing Director' of this, would be that much more tolerable with an erudite chauffeur and pilot to talk with. He even got as far as thinking about the contract to dissuade Danvers from going off teaching, or some such nonsense, when he had got his degree!

After such excitement there was silence for a while. Middlesex ruminated, as visions of Sir Galahads in Green Rabbit armour, and Holy Grails that had R.A.C. stamped all over them, floated in and out of consciousness. Dasha attempted to draw what they had seen on the notepad thoughtfully provided on each arm-rest. Sergei was full of helpful suggestions, which were not gratefully received, and in the end he drew his version of the Corn Rabbit and labelled it as best he could. Their reveries were broken by Danvers.

"London ahead, Sir Magnus."

They looked out of their windows again, down at the twinkling wonder of a city illuminated by energy gleaned from an ancient, younger sun. Massive tower blocks looked like punched cards, a light in every hole. Ordered loops of blue or orange glow marked the transport arteries, and the moving headlights of cars flowed like silver blood. And sprinkled through the myriads of earth-bound stars were black holes, vortices of unimaginable power and horror. They saw the Thames glittering reflected diamonds, and the dully glowing face of Big Ben. Then, slowly, the density of trapped star-dust began to thin out, and the face of the river darkened.

"Approaching Tilbury, Sir," Danvers called out, and within minutes they were out over the Thames estuary. The waters were charcoal now, yet still possessing a metallic glow broken only by the odd white-cap. Red and green pin-points of light marked the tiny capsules, in which the lords of the earth dared to skate the surface of that vast empire in which they are the aliens.

Danvers turned the craft north over Southend and Clacton, Ipswich and Felixstowe, with their gay splashes of defiance to the night sky. On over Aldeburgh and past the nuclear power station at Sizewell. Then darkness, punctuated by only an odd bright comma or full-stop, marking isolated hamlets and homes.

"Do you think, Sir Magnus," Middlesex asked tentatively, "that I might take over the controls for a few minutes - under Mr Danvers' direction, of course?"

"All right, Danvers?" asked Sir Magnus.

"Yes, of course, Sir," Danvers replied half-heartedly. He asked himself what could go wrong if he was there to look after things - and funked the answer!

Middlesex moved up front and took Danvers' seat, and his pilot's cap. "Now, please show me the controls, Mr Danvers. This really is capital - better than the Rolls, even."

Danvers hesitated, until Sir Magnus said: "Get on with it, Danvers. Nothing can possibly go wrong."

So Danvers showed Middlesex how to go into a climb, hold the craft steady, go into a dive, flap control, and how the retractable undercarriage worked. The steady throb of the engine, the feel of the joystick; above all, the sensation of limitless freedom was too much for Middlesex. A powerful wave of G-R-I-D drowned reason and banished caution. The plane was put into a steep climb.

"Steady on, dear friend," Sir Magnus called, fastening his seat belt and motioning the twins to do likewise. "Bring her down a bit."

"Orders received and understood," Middlesex shouted joyfully. "Roger, over and out," and immediately put the plane into an even steeper dive.

"Take over, Danvers," Sir Magnus ordered quietly. "Dammit, at once!"

But Middlesex was not to be moved. Danvers could only lean over and grab the joystick. He managed to level the plane out at five hundred feet, but at the price of a sudden and sizeable lurch. Not being strapped into a seat, Danvers was knocked off balance and fell sideways. His head caught the control panel and he fell to the deck unconscious.

Fortunately, a great deal of Sir Magnus's success in business was his ability to 'keep his cool'.

"Just fly a steady course at this height, dear friend," he called, unperturbed. "No cause for panic. Here, you two, give me a hand."

The twins, thoroughly shaken, undid their safety belts with trembling hands and went up front. Together with Sir Magnus, they managed to get Danvers on to one of the chairs.

Sir Magnus glanced briefly out of one of the windows. "Lowestoft below, we're dead on course."

"I hope we're not," said Sergei. "Dead, that is!"

Sir Magnus laughed, always at his best in a crisis. "Don't worry," he said gently. "I know enough to get us down safely. Watched Danvers do it a thousand times." Then his attention turned to the 'pilot'. "Hold her steady," he called. "We'll turn inland over Yarmouth in a few minutes."

Meanwhile, he administered brandy to the still limp Danvers; Sergei slapped his hands and Dasha wet a towel in the tiny hand-basin and laid it across his forehead.

They were all too busy to be aware what Middlesex was doing, so that they were not to know that in Middlesex's head G-R-I-D had been dismissed by G-R-I-L and G-R-A-S-S. It was noted, by these life preservers, that the tide was well out; that there was a great stretch of firm and gleaming sand ahead and that, after the pier, there were no obstructions. Gently, the plane began to lose height.

Sir Magnus, when he saw Danvers' eyes beginning to open and the colour return to his face, left him to the ministrations of the twins and went up front to help Middlesex turn inland. Instead, he saw the sand coming up to meet them through the cock-pit window.

"What in carnation...?!" he finally exploded. There was a soft bounce as the wheels made first contact with the sand, then another and another, until they were running smoothly along it. Middlesex applied the brakes and they came to an imperceptible halt. Middlesex leaned back and sighed a sigh of perfect bliss, and silently thanked G-R-I-L and G-R-A-S-S for their timely intervention.

Up on the promenade holiday makers, out for a bedtime stroll, clapped and cheered the perfect landing.

"Well done, my friend," said Sir Magnus, full of admiration. "Well done! A perfect landing and all that. Truly fantastic!"

"Merely an example of what G-R-I-L and G-R-A-S-S can do," Middlesex modestly replied. "But how is my dear friend, Mr Danvers?"

"I'm fine now," Danvers replied quickly on his own behalf. And indeed he was, not that he knew they were once more down safely on terra-firma. "It was nothing really. I'm perfectly fit to fly us all home now."

"Later," said Sir Magnus. "Right now, I think some refreshment is called for."

As they clambered out of the plane, there was a brief altercation with the Law, but the name of Sir Magnus de Verte, and a promise to be gone within the hour, cleared the air.

Sir Magnus led the little party towards his favourite four-star hotel, but then the twins smelt the 'chippie'.

"Please, Sir Magnus," said Dasha, in her most appealing voice and with her most disarming smile, "do we have to go to a posh hotel? We're not really dressed for it."

"Don't worry, my dear," Sir Magnus began. "There'll be no trouble about..."

"Please, couldn't we just get some chips and pop?" Sergei interrupted, his mouth already watering. "It'd cost less anyway."

Sir Magnus hesitated, looking at the anxious expressions on the twins' faces. "Very well then, it's your outing, after all," he relented. "I must confess to the sad fact that I have never been to a... a..."

"A chippie!" Dasha helped him out. "Oh thank you, Sir Magnus!"

Sir Magnus turned to Middlesex. "I hope you don't mind, my friend! This has proved to be a night for new experiences, so a chippie will be appropriate."

"I'm happy whatever you decide," Middlesex replied, still in a state of euphoria. "But I'll just have peas, if you don't mind!"

So, fifteen minutes later, the five of them, with socks and shoes off, walked along the edge of a gentle sea. The tiny wavelets lazily cascaded over four pairs of naked feet and one pair of green, furry paws.

They left behind them no footsteps in the wet sand, but an aromatic trail of vinegar and frying marked their passing. Picking his liberally salted and doused chips delicately out of their brown paper wrapping, Sir Magnus experienced the incommunicable joy of the right food at the right time in the right place. He marveled that the 'French-fries' that has accompanied many an expensive steak or exotic fish delicacy had never tasted as did those chips on Yarmouth sands.

As the moon came up over the sea, Danvers lifted the plane smoothly from its sandy runway and touched down as smoothly thirty minutes later, on the grassy runway on the old airfield. When the twins and Middlesex climbed sleepily out of the Rolls at the gate of WORLD'S END, Sir Magnus leaned out. "Thank you so much," he said "for teaching me to live again. It has been quite exhilarating and all that..."

Middlesex beamed with Green Rabbit contentment: "Capital, just capital! Together we can make the world anew - green and vivid and fresh! Goodnight, Sir Magnus, and thank you!"

"Yes, thank you very much!" the twins shouted, as they ran after the green glow bounding up the garden path to the front door.

CHAPTER VII

To release the spring of laughter is to release the spring of renewal.
(B. O. P. Bk. 2)

Monday dawned a perfect day, so the Polenskis rose early. The Captain wanted to cut the lawn before it got too hot, and Mrs Polenski felt the same way about the household chores. So after a seven o'clock breakfast of orange juice and apples, it was mutually decided that the aim should be to complete all tasks by noon. After which they would eat before preparing themselves, mentally and physically, for the rigours of the festivities. Middlesex raked the lawn in the wake of the rotary cutter and washed the Captain's car. Mrs Polenski swept through the house like an avenging angel and the twins tactfully kept out of her way, up in the attic, putting final touches to their costumes.

The sun swung higher in the sky, draining colour and energy from the landscape and its inhabitants. By the time the family assembled for lunch under the conker tree, they were full of satisfaction at their virtuous efforts but drained of all vitality. It was too hot to be profound so the table talk was light and banal, and sleep claimed them, one by one, as their appetites were satiated. It was the time to the siesta, and the used pots and cutlery lay unheeded on the grass.

Middlesex was the first to wake up, roused by an insistent cry from G-R-I-L, that it was time for a rough synopsis to be attempted. Time for all the divergent theories and observations to be linked in coherent one. Slowly and carefully, taking care to disturb not even the flies that were now gorging themselves on the empty plates, Middlesex went in to the comparative cool of the cottage. Borrowing Dasha's sketching pad and Sergei's thick black pencil, the first draft of G-R-A-F-T was committed to paper:

G___ R____ A_____ F____ T__
GREEN RABBIT ARISTOCRATIC FAMILY TREE

ANCIENT CULT OF GREEN RABBIT. (THE THEN DOMINANT SPECIES OF GENUS LEPUS.) MUCH HUNTED BY NEOLITHIC MAN FOR ITS EXCELLENT MEAT, SKIN AND FUR; EASIER PREY THAN WILD BOAR ETC. AN INVALUABLE SOURCE OF PROTEIN. PEOPLES OF PRE-HISTORY HAD THE COURTESY TO ACKNOWLEDGE THEIR DEBT TO THEIR PREY BY ARTISTIC REPRESENTATIONS, E. G. CAVE PAINTINGS AND THREE DIMENSIONAL EARTHWORK SCULPTURES.

THOUGH HUNTED TO NEAR EXTINCTION AND RARELY SEEN AFTER ROMAN OCCUPATION, RACIAL MEMORIES AWAKENED WHEN KING EDMUND WAS ADOPTED AS THE RALLYING POINT AGAINST VIKING AND DANISH AGGRESSION. THIS REGENERATION OF THE WILL TO RESIST WAS A "GREEN" ACT, THEREFORE HE HAS COME DOWN THROUGH THE CENTURIES AS THE GREEN KING. POSSIBLE LINK ALSO BETWEEN LEGEND THAT IT WAS A WOLF WHO GUARDED HIS SEVERED HEAD AND WOLFBANE OR ACONITE - PECULIAR TO EAST ANGLIA.

MEDIEVAL MYSTERY PLAYS UNCONSCIOUSLY ADOPTED THE MARTYRDOM OF EDMUND FOR A GREEN MAN CHARACTER, TO SYMBOLIZE REBIRTH AND REGENERATION. ALSO, CHRIST DIED ON A TREE ON A GREEN HILL.

LATER, THE LITTLE FOLK WHO, IF TREATED HONOURABLY, COULD PROSPER INDIVIDUAL LIVES, E. G. LEPRECHAUNS, BUGGANES, TROLLS – OFTEN THOUGHT OF AS GREEN OR BATHED IN GREEN LIGHT.

MODERN - RABBIT PAWS ADOPTED AS GOOD LUCK CHARMS.

SECOND WORLD WAR - OUTLINE OF THE "CORN RABBIT" SEEN BY AIRMEN WHEN FLYING AND ADOPTED AS THEIR MASCOT.

ME (?)

A warm surge of achievement enveloped Middlesex as the signature, G-R-I-L, was appended in outsize Capitals, with a few flourishes for good measure.

It was now half-past three, so Middlesex returned to the garden to wake the others, determined that the blessings of G-R-I-L should be at the service of this adoptive family, who were such worthy candidates. When everyone was fully conscious again, and had consumed vast quantities of iced fruit juice, Middlesex nobly offered to do the washing-up, if Mrs Mum's rubber gloves could be borrowed to protect green fur. Just as the last glass was being carefully wiped, Mrs Mum called Middlesex up to the attic. She was dressed in Polish national costume, gay and beribboned. She shut the door firmly and whispered: "I've got a surprise for you, and the twins know nothing about it either.... I've concocted a costume for you. I hope you don't mind!"

"On the contrary," Middlesex grinned, "But what can you do with a rabbit my shape and size and colour, Mrs Mum?"

"Why do you call me Mrs Mum?" she asked, as she delved into the back of the wall cupboard.

"I do hope you don't mind," Middlesex answered shyly. "It's less formal and... if I may presume to say it, it makes me feel a kind of a part of your family."

"Of course I don't mind. That is just what I would like you to feel," she said warmly, as she turned round and displayed what she had on the hanger. But the disjointed costume made no sense to Middlesex, or to G-R-I-L for that matter.

"Come on," Mrs Polenski said eagerly, and she fed green arms into a richly embroidered scarlet waistcoat. Then she eased on a golden satin cut-away coat, with lace sewn in at the wrists and neck. Finally she balanced a tall, grey hat between the large ears.

"I can't swear to the strict historical accuracy of the costume," she said laughing, "but pick up your ebony and silver stick and look in the mirror!"

Middlesex complied, staring at the reflection with instant and unreserved approval. "This is most assuredly G-R-A-N-D, which translates to, if you remember, Green Rabbit Approved 'N' Desired."

"But do you get it?" Mrs Polenski asked smiling, "Do you see the pun?"

"The pun, Mrs Mum?" Middlesex enquired, puzzled.

"Yes ," she laughed. "Just for today, one of your problems is resolved. You are a Buck - a Regency Buck!"

Middlesex roared with laughter. "You're a genius, Mrs Mum, a genius! This is one of the most memorable moments of my life. I must go and show the twins. Capital, just capital!"

The descent down the stairs was suspiciously like a series of bunny hops. "Sergei! Dasha! Come and look at me. Come and see what your wonderful, clever mum has made for me!"

Dasha appeared. "Gosh," she said. "Oh Middlesex, you look smashing. But what are you exactly?"

"I'm a Buck - A Regency Buck," Middlesex said proudly. Dasha looked apprehensive. "Are you really a buck then, Middlesex? Does this mean that you're not a 'middle-sex' anymore?"

"No, of course not." Middlesex was suddenly serious. "That is a mystery that goes deeper than borrowed plumes."

The seriousness passed as swiftly as it had come. "But for today I am a Buck at the Court of Prinny, the Prince Regent! The greatest Dandy of them all. I am Beau Brummel!"

Dasha laughed, reassured. "You sound like Scarlet O'Hara in *Gone with the Wind*. I know, will you be my beau for today?"

"The pleasure, Madam, will be mine," Middlesex replied gallantly, and offered Dasha an elegant arm. "I shall be proud to be seen escorting such a pretty bunny."

And Dasha did, indeed, look pretty in her frilly dress and white bob-tail, her floppy ears, made from the fur fabric lining of an old gabardine, framing her face.

Then Sergei appeared, *10s/6d* stuck on the side of his old topper, and sporting a set of whiskers culled from the black nylon bristles of a hand brush.

"Cor luv-a-duck! what is this I see before mine eyes!" Sergei laughed. "I say, you really do look good. But it's crazy, man, crazy! I'm a hare, Dasha's a bunny, and you're a human. I'll soon be having a bad attack of G-R-I-M, which freely translated reads Green Rabbit Instant Madness."

The Captain emerged from his bedroom. He was togged out in white flying overalls, a skull cap supporting two silver antennae topped by tiny stars, and *U. F. O. RESCUE SERVICE* in bold black letters across his chest and back.

"Will all aliens please step forward," he said, laughing at the spectacle before him.

"Doesn't Middlesex look smashing?" Dasha asked.

"Almost human," teased her father.

"And there's a two-edged compliment, if ever I heard one," said Mrs Polenski coming down the stairs. "But come along everyone, it's getting late and I don't want to miss one moment of this 'Happening'."

As they piled into the car, Middlesex and Sergei struggling with their hats, the twins were already arguing as to what Sir Magnus would be wearing.

They arrived on the Green just after seven o'clock, to find Sir Magnus poised to welcome his multitude of guests. He was standing on the steps of the war memorial, resplendent in the flowing white robes of a Roman Senator. His toga was edged with the Royal Putjie, and his silver hair was crowned with a wreath of laurel. When he saw the arrival of Middlesex and the Polenskis, he waved excitedly, until they went and stood to either side of him. Then he held up his hand in magnificent senatorial style. "My friends!" and his voice rang out across the now silent crowd.

"My dear friends! I am delighted to see you all here, and to welcome you warmly to our Midsummer Festival. Forty-eight hours ago this idea, to celebrate the summer solstice in the traditional way, came to me when I met, for the first time, an exhilarating individual," and he placed one arm round Middlesex's shoulders, "when this 'fact is stranger than fiction' character exploded into my life! And let me assure you, dear friends, that once you have known a Green Rabbit, your life will never be the same again. So, if the Bard of Avon will forgive me, I say: 'I come to praise Middlesex: not to bury him in twentieth century disbelief'. Now, eat, drink and be merry, my friends, so that these children, waiting here with patient impatience," and he waved vaguely in the direction of Sergei and Dasha, "will so mark this day that they will tell their children, and their children's children, of the day when the people of Farthingale Inferior rediscovered the magic of The Green Rabbit!"

The sophisticated crowd of modern, 'swinging' English found such naive enthusiasm somewhat embarrassing, and there was a brief awkward pause. Then a handful of guests heard a little girl say "I like green rabbits, 'cos they're cuddly!" They laughed, the tension broke; and Sir Magnus got his applause, even as young Tubble spun the tum-table and *I've Got a Brand-New Combine Harvester* spilled out of the strategically placed loudspeakers.

Dasha claimed her beau again and they wandered off, while the Captain and his wife drifted over to sample Mr Tubble's potent fruit punch with Sir Magnus. Sergei 'hared' off with some of his school friends to the darts and the bowling for a pig. The party was under way! Robin Hoods were fathers to little spacemen, lion tamers and Noddys. Bold pirates escorted Queen Boadicea, a can-can girl and the Statue of Liberty. A diminutive Alice-in-

Wonderland trailed after a buxom Scheherazade; and Henry the Eighth had a seventh wife on his arm, an over-developed belly-dancer. Green Rabbits had proliferated everywhere and their companions ranged from hula-hula girls to Queen Victoria; from Mrs Alf Garnet, complete with curlers, to fairy godmothers. Bug-eyed monsters danced with Geisha girls, and the Loch Ness Monster accompanied The Queen of Sheba. Danvers, an absent-minded professor with an outsize pair of the proverbial spectacles tangled in his hair, forgot to be serious, and flirted with Mae West and Joan of Arc. Mr Grundy, true to his calling, was a 'Nut and Bolt Case' in a horizontally-striped T-shirt and a big cardboard nut round his waist. Even P.C. Bill, who was off duty, had risen to the heights of a Sherlock Holmes disguise. Back at the Police house, P.C. Ted fulfilled his duties sitting in the doorway, his plastered leg resting on a chair, so that he could observe the scene. Mr Tubble, steaming gently in the still powerful sun, ladled out his fruit punch by the gallon, resplendent as a Victorian bar-man in striped shirt, expanding arm-bands, white boater and white apron. Young Tubble performed his duties in troubadour costume, a non-electric cardboard lute strung across his back.

So the late afternoon perspired into the cool of the evening. The Grand Parade was held, and the winners promised an aerial picnic in Sir Magnus's plane. Groups formed and dispersed; the floor shows added to the merriment in odd corners of the Green; dancing broke out as the evening breeze blew energy back into the young and not-so-young. Food and drink flowed like manna down throats large and small.

At dusk the fairy lights were switched on, lending eerie enchantment to the trembling leaves of sycamore, oak and ash through which they hung. As shadows lengthened, unlikely couples wandered hand-in-hand into the intimate pools of darkness beyond the trees. Over the loud speakers young Tubble matched the mellowing mood with *Save All Your Kisses For Me* and selections from *South Pacific*. People sat around on the grass watching the stars come to radiance in the darkening sky, and even the children were quieter. Sir Magnus, always the perfect host, wandered from group to group inviting his guests to eat yet more food, drink yet more wine, exchanging light banter laced with the occasional touch of profundity.

The Captain lay sprawled on the grass, his arm around his wife, and tried not to worry about Middlesex's disappearance. The twins were searching for Itself in a desultory fashion, but took the opportunity for a rest each time they came to a group containing one of their friends.

Early on, Dasha and Middlesex had wandered over to the far side of the duck-pond, recently cleaned out by the local environmental group, which supported a respectable population of coots, moorhens, ducks and even a pair of geese. As the trees were on the far side of the pond and as there were no houses near it, the pond's bank was the location of the firework display. So it was here that Mr Perkins, suitably turned out as Guy Fawkes, had excelled himself in his pyromaniac art. A huge wire screen had been erected, and a number of suitable motifs tastefully executed. Middlesex immediately recognised the familiar shape of the centre attraction, but to Dasha it was all pretty much of a muddle, and she took no further interest in it. Later on, noticing the dozen or so Green Rabbits present, Middlesex fell prey to G-R-I-D and, during one of Dasha's many excursions to the ice-cream stall, had surreptitiously escaped. One by one, the Green Rabbits were taken to one side by their natural leader, the plan explained and their co-operation secured. As darkness fell, they assembled in the small builder's yard which one of them owned, in the High Street. Under cover of darkness, they transported ladders and scaffolding to the edge of the duck-pond without being noticed. Then, on Middlesex's direction, they erected a series of platform shelves, as far back from the firework screen as the pond would allow. Then they drifted back to their family groups, and no one was any the wiser.

Middlesex re-joined the Captain and Mrs Polenski. "Oh, there you are!" the Captain exclaimed with relief. "The twins are looking for you."

"I'm so sorry," said Middlesex apologetically. "I had a little matter that needed my attention."

The Captain nodded, but was uneasy at the twinkle in those dark eyes. When the June night was as dark as it would get, and as the moon rose like a ripe Cheshire cheese over the horizon, the music died away. Then Sir Magnus's voice drifted on the warm breeze to all his guests.

"It is the time now to admire the Grand Firework display, heroically conceived and executed by our good friend, Mr Guy Fawkes – alias Mr Perkins!" A ripple of laughter ran through the crowd, and the children rediscovered their energy. "May I take this opportunity of thanking you all for humouring my whim, and making this the Midsummer Night of the century. After the display some of you may like to take your youngsters home, but there will be music and dancing, and a barbecue, for as far into the night as you choose. Thank you!"

This time the applause was spontaneous, enthusiastic and prolonged.

Then slowly everyone drifted to the far end of the Green - and waited expectantly.

Guy Fawkes, full of punch and beer, entered into his role with a will and crept conspiratorially about his work, letting forth gurgles of evil laughter as he lit the blue touch papers. During all the excitement, as Roman candles glowed, Catherine wheels spun and rockets roared, the Green Rabbit Brigade made their escape unremarked.

Finally, Mr Perkins came to his *piece de resistance*, the huge figure in the centre of the display screen. He allowed everything to die down, let the crowd experience the depth of darkness with eyes dilated by the brilliant flashes of his lesser creations. Then, with a blood-curdling yell, he pressed the switch that would automatically spark all the touch papers simultaneously. And suddenly, over Farthingale Green, flared a gigantic Green Rabbit: its nose a Catherine wheel, its outline green Roman candles, the whiskers lines of intense white light, and the pointed ears topped by two gigantic rockets timed to go up a few seconds later.

Its size, its intensity, above all its sudden emergence drew a sharp gasp from the onlookers. Then its very brilliance, like a laser-key, seemed to unlock some long-forgotten racial memory and reverence hung in the air. As eyes became accustomed to the splendour of light, an excited murmur gathered momentum to find final release in an explosion of cheering and clapping. For now could be seen the eerily illumined figures of Green Rabbits in the empty spaces of the flaring form; supernatural forces materializing out of the drifting green smoke!

On the highest bit of scaffolding, the face of Middlesex appeared, filling in the vacancy of the forehead. Fancy dress discarded now, the greenness of the glow from Itself vied with that of the fireworks.

The touch paper on the rockets glowed a dull red. Then, as with a great roar they shot skywards, Middlesex jumped, arms and paws fully extended. The coiled impetus from the big haunches lifted Itself high above the display. Middlesex seemed to hang there suspended, motionless, a 'green' presence of illimitable power and vitality, which flooded every mind. The rockets exploded far above, and showers of glittering snow cascaded down as Middlesex came crashing down on the top step of the scaffolding. The great thumpers landed on it with too great a velocity and weight. The whole edifice tottered, swayed, keeled over backwards and, collapsing, deposited the whole Green Rabbit Brigade into the duck pond.

There was a stunned silence before a cacophony of spluttering voices, ducks quacking, geese gaggling and coots protesting broke forth. Green Rabbit relatives ran to the pond to fish out their loved ones, but the rest of the pantomime crowd, merry on Mr Tubble's offerings and suddenly released from an unexpected and profound experience, burst out in an orgy of laughter that was even heard by folk in Farthingale Superior, two miles down the road. Within minutes it had infected both victims and worried relatives alike, as though a sudden plague had struck the revellers. Cavemen and Abraham Lincoln, artists and Red Indians, Churchills and mermaids gasped for breath. Tears rolled down the faces of Lord High Executioners, clowns, pearly queens and Indian fakirs. Hercules, shepherds, Spanish senoritas and cowboys rolled over on the grass in paroxysms, holding stomachs and sides that ached with the force of the uncontrollable hilarity.

Very much later, Middlesex gained sufficient control to shake the water out of bedraggled green fur, unable to peel it off as the others were doing. Itself looked around and saw Sir Magnus sitting on the grass, a crumpled Caesar with his laurel crown askew, still shaken sporadically by a further giggle. Middlesex walked over to him, a little unsure, for G-R-I-L had delivered a reprimand for the prank, but G-R-A-S-S had been all re-assurance.

"I hope, Sir Magnus," Middlesex began politely, sitting down beside him, "I hope that I have not ruined your spectacle."

Sir Magnus turned, wiped the tears from his eyes, and regarded the unpredictable. Unwillingly, because his sides were so tender, he began to laugh again. "Oh, my dear friend, my dear friend," he gasped at last, "It was magnificent; you were magnificent; truly magnificent!"

The incident seemed to revive appetites and increase thirst; and so the merry-making went on until the pale light from the East heralded another perfect day.

The Captain, however, had to face the fact of a return to duty within a few hours, so he took his little party home around two o'clock. The twins slept-walked in and out of the car, and eventually fell onto their beds fully-dressed, to remain there unconscious for the next eight hours. The Captain smiled down tenderly at his wife, who had been asleep even before her head touched the pillow. For himself, he remained conscious long enough to reset his alarm clock, with a deep feeling of gratitude to Sir Magnus, who had offered to let Danvers fly him up to London so he could steal an extra three hours sleep after experiencing the most extra-ordinary weekend of a frequently extraordinary life.

CHAPTER VIII

As Earth rotates to the rising sun, thoughts rotate to the inward flame, and one becomes.
(B. O. P. Bk. 3)

No one noticed that Middlesex did not go up to bed also. At the front door, the night scents asserted their power and Green Rabbit whiskers quivered. The reality of the nocturnal world beckoned one of its own. Itself walked slowly across the garden, vaulted the white barred gate, then, with pace quickening, steps evolved into hops.

G-R-A-S-S took command. Through sleeping fields of corn, where the inhabitants of that other night-time world went through the rituals of life - playing, eating, mating, giving birth and dying - Middlesex followed G-R-A-S-S. Over dry ditches, along banks and hedgerows, where nests and dens and lairs were the scenes of great activity, to lanes no longer the domain of lethal machines that dealt daily death to so many small creatures. Middlesex travelled fast, for G-R-A-S-S was an unerring guide, and willingly, for G-R-I-L had worked out the only possible destination.

So Itself came to the vast complex of fields that, at ground level, kept the ancient secret intact. Sitting upright on green haunches, Middlesex faced the east and waited. The sky was paling over the ridge of gently rising ground. In a little copse to the right, a single bird note fluttered in the stillness. As though it had been waiting for such a signal, the cool breeze of dawn rippled through the corn and whispered an answer. The bird called again, and again, until a different note sounded. Soon the grey-pearled sky drew vitality from the growing song, and colour brushed the soft low clouds. The conversationalists grew more numerous: greetings were exchanged and news broadcast, arguments flared briefly and assignations were arranged, as the dawn chorus rendered its impromptu oratorio. The sky brightened; soon its fiery Lord and master would begin his long ascent to high noon. The chattering birds quietened as they, too, awaited the return of the source of all life. Middlesex, aware of every movement, of every nuance of sound, waited too on this Midsummer morning, secure at last in this spiritual home. A glow capped the ridge, and with slow majesty the rim of the red orb broke into consciousness. Middlesex closed those wonderful velvet eyes and with head bowed, listened to G-R-I-L. When the full circle was complete and rested briefly on the ridge, the green head raised itself, the eyes opened, and Middlesex was content.

It was time to leave.

Middlesex returned to WORLD'S END at a leisurely pace, arriving just before the milkman. Tip-toeing into the sitting room, Itself took up Dasha's sketch pad and tore off the draft copy of G-R-A-F-T. On the next sheet Middlesex wrote, what G-R-I-L dictated.

MY DEAR FAMILY, G-R-I-L TELLS ME THAT I MUST LEAVE WORLD'S END FOR A LITTLE WHILE. THIS DAWN I VISITED THE GREEN RABBIT OF THE FIELDS AND WATCHED THE SUN REBORN. MY QUEST MUST CONTINUE BUT I HAVE FOUND TWO ANSWERS HERE AT WORLD'S END.
FIRSTLY: I HAVE FOUND A LONG AND HONOURABLE LINEAGE, AND I LEAVE WITH YOU THE FIRST COPY OF A GREEN RABBIT ARISTOCRATIC FAMILY TREE. NO DOUBT AS TIME PASSES G-R-I-L WILL EXTEND AND REFINE IT IN THE LIGHT OF FRESH DISCOVERIES.
SECONDLY: I HAVE LEARNT THE ART OF TRUE HAPPINESS: THE WARMTH OF YOUR ACCEPTANCE AND AFFECTION. I SHALL RETURN AGAIN WHEN THE LEAVES ARE SCARLET AND GOLD. FOR THE PRESENT, G-R-I-L ADVISES THAT WE ALL NEED TIME TO REFLECT AND ASSIMILATE. TELL THE TWINS G-R-I-L HAS BEEN HAVING SOME VERY INTERESTING THOUGHTS ABOUT

GHOST-HUNTING. HALLOWE'EN MIGHT BE AN APPROPRIATE THE FOR MAXIMUM RESULTS.

TILL WE MEET AGAIN, MIDDLESEX R.A.C.

P. S. PLEASE PASS ON MY DEEPEST REGARDS TO SIR MAGNUS AND TELL HIM THAT HE IS, MOST TRULY, A CAPITAL FELLOW!

Middlesex re-read the letter and then put it, along with G-R-A-F-T on the kitchen table. There the family were sure to see it at breakfast. Then, taking the ebony and silver stick, Itself went out through the front door and shut it softly. After turning briefly for a last look at the sleeping cottage, and blowing it a kiss from a green, furry paw, Middlesex followed G-R-A-S-S without demur, across fields still cool with dew.

To their surprise, the family found that they were not sad when they read Middlesex's letter. They could look forward eagerly to the return, which was strange because none of them felt that Itself was really gone. They skimmed through G-R-A-F-T together.

"I shall study it when I'm home again," the Captain said, still pressed for time even though he was flying up to London.

Mrs Polenski, hurriedly and a little blearily sewing a button on his shirt, said,"I shall start studying it very carefully today. Even on a quick glance, I can see that there's a lot of reading and research to be done before Middlesex comes back again!"

"I don't know," the Captain said pensively, "I think perhaps Middlesex's problems are best solved by Middlesex."

"I quite agree," said Mrs Polenski to everybody's surprise. "I don't mean psychology and all that nonsense. No, I mean I must read up on ley-lines, and the symbols of regeneration."

The Captain winked at the twins. "That's a jolly good idea. You'll probably be able to help Middlesex a great deal that way."

"And I'm going to find some books on archaeology," Dasha joined in.

Sergei was quick to seize the opportunity, which had just presented itself, to acquire a new toy. "Hey, Dad," he said hopefully, "don't you think it might be helpful if we had a metal detector?"

As Farthingale Inferior came back to life that morning, there were many respectable headaches around in the village, and the shop did a brisk trade in 'hangover' remedies. But none of them matched the non-alcoholic one which afflicted Fred Crumble, the editor of the local 'rag' in Westbury. When he had arrived at his desk that morning, he was confronted by a letter purporting to come from a Green Rabbit. It was written all in capitals, and extolled the efficiency of Police, Fire and Ambulance services in a fire which had not been otherwise reported in Farthingale Inferior. Then there was a long, incredible report from the correspondent in that village, about a spectacular Midsummer party and the antics of a large, upright, talking Green Rabbit! Fred Crumble was not renowned for his sense of humour at the best of times, and this was not the best of times - the weather was too hot, and the circulation figures for the last month were down again.

He looked at the letter again. It bore the address of the mad Captain Polenski, the man who believed in U. F. Os. "It must be a hoax," Fred Crumble told himself, but then forced himself to look at the correspondent's report again. It spoke of Sir Magnus's involvement with, and friendship for, this blasted animal. Fred Crumble swallowed pills and floundered in a sea of indecision. It must be a hoax, he kept telling himself firmly, but the quiet, insistent voice of self-preservation cautioned him that Sir Magnus was, after all, the proprietor of the newspaper. Although Sir Magnus never bullied his subordinates, Fred Crumble was happier believing that he was under constant threat of dismissal. It made his ulcers easier to bear. So that little voice droned on, if Sir Magnus's new friend was ignored or slighted, Sir Magnus might want to know why. After an hour's agony, a delightful ten minutes spent berating his secretary, and three cups of milk, Fred Crumble's keen newspaper man's mind presented a possible solution. He picked up the phone and got through to Farthingale Hall. Progressing from butler to secretary, he finally managed to get through to his Lord and master.

"Good morning, Fred," Sir Magnus whispered. Even the sound of his own voice was too much. "Speak softly, will you, and don't give me any cause to laugh. I am in a very delicate condition."

Fred Crumble committed his future to the tone of his voice, and whispered back, "Would you please tell me, Sir Magnus... I have a report on my desk of a party in the village yesterday, but it is not clear if..." He paused and sent up a newspaper man's prayer - "It's not clear if the Green Rabbit is Middlesex or a lady - or titled, perhaps?"

Sir Magnus fought back the temptation to laugh, not because of Fred Crumble's sensitive nature, but because of his own tenderness. All he would allow himself was a very satisfied grin as he whispered back: "There's no handle to the name, Fred, no handle. Just Middlesex R.A.C. It is enough!"

- 0 - 0 - 0 - 0 - 0 -

Part Two – Hallowe'en

A wall is no barrier to an enterprising spirit
Book of Proverbs (G-R-A-V)

CHAPTER IX

A leap in the dark can be the first step to enlightenment
(B. O. P. Bk. 2)

Middlesex waited. The silver chain, dangling the R.A.C. medallion, lay on the green chest with mayoral dignity. Vibrant yet drowsy, the furrowed fields sprawled in late October sunshine. Red hip and crimson haw glowed a rich harvest for birds busy with ratty insurance against the lean months of winter.

Middlesex waited, ears tall and alert, by the little one-armed signpost, fringed by dry candelabras of hog-weed and cow parsley. Soon the vigil ended, as the sound of laughter preceded the twins as they ran down the lane from the school-bus stop. Discerning ears picked up the crackle of leaves, scattered in a mad search for acorn and conker ammunition. Itself smiled slyly, hastily collected an arsenal of nutty missiles, took cover behind the signpost, and waited.

Sergei was the first to receive a direct hit on the shoulder blade from the Second Front. Before he had really registered it, a tattoo of conkers ricocheted off his anorak even as Dasha caught him, face on, in a flight of acorns. He jumped aside smartly onto the grass verge, turning to see who it was attacking from the rear. As his eyes searched the deserted road, noting the absence of cover in the austere forest of dried stalks and frost-wilted grass, a suspicion formed and grew hopefully.

He studied the diminutive white signpost, still some three metres away, with narrowed eyes. Even at this distance, it seemed to Sergei, the hard line of its upright post was fuzzed by a green haze. Then, as Dasha came running towards him, he signalled her to silence and pointed to the signpost.

"Something... somebody was pelting me in the back with little conkers," he whispered urgently.

Dasha's eyes met his. "Middlesex?"

Sergei nodded. "Collect as many nuts as you can. Pretend you're still playing, but work your way up this side. I'll circle round the other, and we'll get Itself fair and square!"

Dasha ran obligingly to the next oak tree shouting loudly, "Ouch! I'll get you for that," as she stuffed her pockets with acorns. With commando-like precision, they at last reached their positions. There was an expectant hush until the battle cry of *Now we've got you!* killed the silence.

A hail of burnished conkers and acorns hurtled up in a sharp parabola, only to fall ineffectually on to the grass between them.

"Splendid! Capital – just capital!" a familiar voice cheered them on. They stopped short, the next handful unlaunched, and looked up.

There sat Middlesex, perched on top of the signpost, twirling the silver-capped ebony-stick.

"I declare it a draw," Itself pronounced, prematurely as it proved, for the twins, with instinctive timing and devastating accuracy, hurled their pellets straight at the green head. Powerful haunches flexed and landed their owner a metre away from the next bombardment. Giggles robbed the victors of their accuracy, and a well-placed leap removed Middlesex from the target area.

"P-A-X?" Itself shouted laughing.

"No, unconditional surrender," Sergei retorted, flicking a last acorn at Middlesex.

Middlesex caught the nut with the side of the ebony stick and sent it flying high into the air. "Never!" came the uncompromising reply.

"And own up, now! You were expecting me today, weren't you?"

"Well, it is October thirtieth!" Dasha's tone implied that the truth was self-evident.

"That's right, and tomorrow is Hallowe'en," Sergei added impatiently. "But no, to be honest, we didn't expect you! To expect means that there could have been some doubt about you turning up. No! I just knew you'd be here like you know you'll get a headache if a cricket ball hits you between the eyes!" He stopped, surprised by his succinct appraisal of the situation – but then Middlesex always had that effect on him.

"And come to think of it, I knew something mind-blowing was going to happen," Dasha added, joining in the tease. "We had green jelly for lunch today."

Middlesex grinned and glowed green delight. "Splendid, capital! I'm home again."

"Where have you been then?" Dasha asked casually.

"And 'hare' goes the quest? Have you made up your mind yet whether you're a HESSEX or a SHESEX?" Sergei added irreverently.

Middlesex shrugged green shoulders. "Oh, I've been here and there. I've travelled far in space and time. G-R-I-L and G-R-A-S-S have plenty of facts and fancies to work on. And I am still MIDDLESEX."

"G-R-I-L? That's Green Rabbit Instant Logic, isn't it?" Sergei remembered triumphantly.

"And G-R-A-S-S! That's Green Rabbit Automatic Sixth Sense," Dasha added. "You see, we haven't forgotten."

"G-R-I-T never imagined that you would, or could," Middlesex retorted.

"Come on, then, let's have it," Sergei shouted. "G-R-I-T?"

"It's Green Rabbit Instant Trust, of course," Middlesex grinned.

"OK, but why is it that for you everything, like trust or logic and desire are always instant or automatic?" Dasha demanded, as they began to amble down the lane to WORLD'S END.

Middlesex twirled the ebony stick, took a gigantic vertical leap to steal a fleeting preview of the cottage, and then launched into an 'instant' homily.

"Well, you see, my friends, it is in the instantaneous –in the spontaneous – that the ancient truths lie. *Consider the lilies of the field*, says your bible. But *no! No!* shout the old gods. Would you smother them in boredom? Gasp at their sudden beauty: smell them, pick them, put them in your hair... but move on. Freshness is of the essence always."

"Sounds like a Persil advert..." Sergei began disrespectfully, embarrassed as always by Middlesex's lapses into profundity.

"Oh, do be quiet!" Dasha snapped at her brother. "Do you mean, Middlesex, that we shouldn't pull things to pieces, and fix each part with a name? 'Cos if you do, I wish you'd tell our botany teacher. I hate pulling flowers to pieces."

Middlesex stopped and gazed pensively at the young people. "For your complicated life-support systems in this technological age, I suppose it is necessary to understand the parts rather than savour the whole. But remember, always, the old ways, and find time for them too; like capital letters, they clarify and redirect the mind."

"And I'm going to re-direct yours!" shouted Sergei. "We're going ghost-hunting tomorrow night. Sir Magnus has invited us all up to the Hall for Hallowe'en."

"Splendid, just capital," Middlesex enthused. "It will be good to see Sir Magnus and Mr Danvers again. And what of dear Mrs Mum and the Captain?"

"Mum and Dad are fine," Dasha said. Mum has gone to pick Dad up in Westbury. He's got four days' leave, but they won't be back for a little while because Mum wants to do the shopping."

"Which means," Sergei added in conspiratorial tones, "that we can investigate behind the fireplace."

Dasha was enthusiastic. "Great! We've got three hours, and we've got Middlesex."

Then they told Itself about their suspicions that there was a hollow space behind the Victorian bookshelves that stood in the alcove to one side of the big, open fireplace in the lounge. Although this aroused many of the Green Rabbit Instant 'things', it took them some time to get Itself indoors. The garden, in its autumnal coat of many colours, had to be re-discovered and its mood savoured. Only when the red glow from a westing sun deepened shade and perspective into meaning was Middlesex content.

"Let us go in," the twins were relieved to hear at last. "G-R-A-S-S promises that the hour is ripe."

So, armed with doughnuts filched from the larder, and celery for Middlesex, they turned their attention to the bookshelves. They removed the books from the shelves and knocked on the back panel. There was a satisfying echo!

"I think it's just wedged in," Sergei announced. "But it's too heavy to budge. Any ideas, Middlesex?"

"I'll go up the chimney," Middlesex offered. "Perhaps I can come down on the other side of it."

"But the soot..." Dasha protested. It was a futile cry, as Middlesex ducked under the great beam which supported the wall over the hearth.

"I can see some footholds higher up," a muffled voice called back.

The green haunches flexed and with a sudden, vertical leap, Middlesex disappeared. There was a moment's silence, a leaden shower of soot, a triumphant shout - and another shower of soot.

"I was right; G-R-A-S-S was right! The wall stops half-way up. I'm going over, and down the other side…"

Another black shower crashed down. Mounds of gossamer black filled the hearth; black snowflakes drifted with soft determination around the room. Then rubble crashed down and sent the gossamer flying in another black blizzard that engulfed the carpet, furniture, walls – and the twins.

"Hey Middlesex, cut it out!" Sergei shouted. "Stop it! We're smothered!"

"Nearly there," came the muffled reply, as another black avalanche crashed down.

"Middlesex!" Dasha screamed. "Middlesex! Oh, Middlesex, stop it! We're smothered."

"Nearly there," came the muffled reply, as another black avalanche crashed down.

"Middlesex!" Dasha screamed. "Middlesex! Oh, Middlesex, stop it! Everything's covered in soot."

The only answer was a victory tattoo hammered out on the back of the bookcase until the shelves rattled. Then came a grating, grinding, ear-splitting crescendo as a gap opened to reveal a five-foot black rabbit, waist deep in soot, emitting a lurid green glow.

"How is that as an example of G-R-I-S, of Green Rabbit Instant Success?" the apparition demanded.

There was no easy, no obvious answer and, for once, even Sergei was speechless. Middlesex, however, was fully in command of the situation.

"Would you get me a torch, Dasha, please. There's a draught up my back."

Dasha did not move. The logic evaded her soot-clouded mind, but Sergei responded.

"Come on, Dasha, a torch! Middlesex wants to warm the nether regions! G-R-I-L them, in fact! Right, you mad black rabbit?"

Middlesex giggled and, after a moment's pause, Sergei followed suit. The tension broke in a whirlpool of laughter as Middlesex stepped through the gap, shaking another maelstrom of black snow into the room.

"Stop it! Stop it!" the twins shouted helplessly. Slowly they returned to dark reality.

"Dad'll skin us alive for this," Sergei bemoaned. "He'll have our H-I-D-E-S for leather gloves!"

Middlesex was unmoved. "I think not," and green-black paws waved airily about. "He will be as intrigued as I am with the tiny passage-way, that leads to a small chamber which is roughly level with the fire back. But our first priority is to get rid of the soot."

Dasha stirred and gazed helplessly at her twin. "I'll get the vac..." she said vaguely.

"No, No!" Middlesex contradicted briskly. "The telephone!"

"But of course!" Sergei did not bother to conceal the sarcasm. "Mum always does the cleaning with the telephone," and he plonked the cream instrument fair and square in Middlesex's black paws. "The end with holes is the suction end!"

Unperturbed, Middlesex dialled the emergency number – nine, nine, nine.

"There has been a dangerous soot fall at World's End, Captain Polenski's residence. Could you please assist us?"

The girl on the switch-board ducked the question, and put the call through to the fire-station. When the situation had been explained, the Fire Chief accepted the challenge gladly. He had been looking for something to occupy his part-time team for their Friday evening training session. This emergency would be an excellent opportunity, also, to try out the new breathing equipment with which they had just been issued. Fortunately, he did not realize who it was at the other end of the line, or he might have opted for the lads jumping out of third-storey windows.

Fifteen minutes later, the Farthingale Inferior Fire Tender followed an impressive Rolls Royce up to the gates of World's End.

Fifteen miles away, Mrs Polenski was innocently purchasing the winter's supply of firelighters at the Cash and Carry, when that most efficient instrument of communication – the rural jungle telegraph – sprang into action. Nigel Gotobed had raced up to the fire station when the fire-siren wailed its dire message over the village. As soon as he heard where they were going, he dashed to the phone and told his wife.

Audrey Gotobed knew where the Polenskis were, as Mrs Polenski had taken Mrs Gotobed Senior into town to do her shopping. So, within twelve minutes of Middlesex's call for help, Audrey Gotobed was speaking to the manager of the Cash and Carry, who speedily found the Polenskis. The only omission in the whole operation was the true reason for the panic, and everyone involved opted for the obvious reason.

The Captain persuaded the old estate car to forget about all speed limits, and his luck held as far as Farthingale Inferior. Then P.C. Wimble doing a leisurely patrol in the Police van narrowly missed plunging into a three-foot ditch as the Captain's car hurtled by. He turned and went off in hot pursuit, having recognised the car, but the Captain was at his gate before the Law caught up with him.

The Captain and his wife stared in bewilderment at their cottage which was ablaze, indeed, but only with lights. They ran up the path, only to stop and stare at a fireman holding a wheelbarrow at the ready outside the lounge window.

"Stefan, what in the world is happening?" Mrs Polenski asked quietly. "Where are the children? What is going on?"

Before the Captain could offer any explanation, P.C. Wimble joined them.

"Captain Polenski, sir, this is a very serious matter. You were doing 65 m.p.h. through the village, and you failed to..."

"Later, Constable, later," the Captain shouted. "Can't you see there's a panic on?"

Taking his wife's hand, he went in through the open front door, and straight to the centre of the hullaballoo which was emanating from the lounge. The unbelievable immobilized them; robbing them of movement, speech, thought even.

The twins, Danvers and sundry firemen, with scarves and handkerchiefs over the lower part of their faces, were piling soot from the fireplace into cardboard cartons. These were then being delivered to the man outside the window and emptied into his wheelbarrow. The Fire Chief, grotesque in full breathing gear, was gesticulating through a hole in the wall, from whence a muffled but rousing chorus of *The Sweep's Song* issued forth. As Mrs Polenski said later, the scene epitomised the morning after of Dante's Inferno.

Suddenly there was a great cry of, "Capital! Just splendid," as a five-foot soot monster, black ears funereally draped over a black face-mask, emerged from the gap. The monster turned and shouted back into the gap, "Sir Magnus, our hosts have arrived. The Captain and dear Mrs Mum are here. What a surprise we have in store for them!"

Animation returned to Mrs Polenski and she groped for the settee, thoughtfully covered over by Dasha with a couple of towels. The rest of the furniture had been draped belatedly with bath-towels, table cloths and sheets. On the floor, torn and crumpled newspapers bore evidence to Dasha's attempts to minimise the disaster.

Sergei and Dasha watched apprehensively as Middlesex bounded across the room, implanted a sooty kiss on their mother's cheek, before grasping the Captain by the hand.

"We have made the most amazing discovery, Captain. Come and see what lies behind your chimney breast."

The Captain regarded his now blackened hand calmly, and followed Middlesex with the quiet resignation of the deeply shocked. But the Fire Chief stopped them.

"Captain Polenski," he began, in an officious tone, "I must inform you that this unblocked cavity behind your bookcase constitutes a major fire hazard. If this quantity of soot were to have ignited, the whole building would have been a write-off."

"But it didn't, and it isn't, my dear fellow!" Sir Magnus pronounced, emerging from the gap and sweeping the Fire Chief to one side. "Now, Captain, do come with us and see what our dear friend, Middlesex, has discovered – or, more succinctly, uncovered."

The Captain was propelled down a two metre-long passage and into a tiny 'hidey-hole'. Middlesex swung the torch round, revealing green walls and a bench across the tar end, on which stood a guttered candle, tinder box, quill pen and some dusty books. Lastly, Middlesex illuminated the ceiling ten centimetres above the Captain's head. And there, standing blackly out on the green ceiling, was a strange motif of three rabbits in a circle, each holding the ear of the rabbit in front in its mouth.

"G-R-A-S-S led me to this," Middlesex said softly. "Forgive me, Captain, Please forgive me."

The Captain, however, was beyond comprehension, let alone compassion, and he allowed himself to be guided out to tile settee on which his wife was sitting. Mrs Polenski looked at her husband, at Middlesex, at Sir Magnus. She gazed round the room at the Black and White Minstrel show, and lastly at her nervous children.

"Dasha," she murmured softly, "be a dear, and make me a cup of tea. In fact, we'd all like a cup of tea, I think."

"A most welcome suggestion," Sir Magnus purred. "I believe our stalwart firemen have all but finished. Everything will soon be ship-shape again."

Mrs Polenski looked round despairingly. "It'll take days – weeks – to clear up this mess."

Sir Magnus sat down gingerly on the sheeted settee. "Two hours at the most, dear lady," he smiled. "My domestic staff should arrive any moment now."

So, while six servants and four vacuum cleaners dealt with the ravages of the holocaust in the lounge, the soot-fighters retired to the kitchen. Hands were washed, gallons of tea were hosed down sooty throats and quantities of cheese sandwiches disposed of. Then Middlesex, who had first been thoroughly hosed down with a vacuum cleaner, and Sir Magnus disappeared behind a chess board. The Fire Chief engaged the Captain in a long and serious discussion on fire hazards in thatched houses, and the twins brought their mother up to date in the Middlesex saga. P.C. Wimble received an unconditional apology from the Captain but, older and wiser than he had been in June, contented himself with pencilling a note in his memo pad: *Oct. 30th 5.30 p.m. Middlesex is back in town.* After which, and innumerable cups of tea, he departed to warn the Station strength of two, and the Sergeant in Westbury, that anything could happen – and probably would!

By ten o'clock the firemen had departed too; the lounge glowed in the light of a log fire – and only the dark gap by the side of the fire-place bore witness to the five traumatic hours of Middlesex's homecoming.

CHAPTER X

Emulation leads to emasculation
(B. O. P. Bk. 3)

Around nine o'clock, Sir Magnus with his usual autocratic benevolence, phoned the Hall and ordered a buffet supper for seven to be sent down to WORLD'S END, along with a change of clothes for himself and Danvers. Then he thanked his staff and spiked their discontent at this extra work, by promising them a bonus in their wage packets. The Polenskis washed and changed too, so that it was a well-scrubbed and tidy party that sat down before the fire of sweet-scented apple logs.

"I hope that you will forgive my impertinence, dear lady," murmured Sir Magnus, as he poured out bowlfuls of celery soup from the vacuum jugs. "I did think, in the circumstances, a prepared meal might be welcome."

Mrs Polenski's grateful amusement spilled over. "Your generosity is matched only by Middlesex's enthusiasm," she purred back. "I am most grateful to you, Sir Magnus; I could not have faced the kitchen stove tonight."

"This is indeed splendid, Capital!" Middlesex pronounced, sniffing the bowl of soup. "And all shall be well and

All manner of things shall be well

When the tongues of flame are infolded

Into the crowned knot of fire

And the fire and the Rabbit are one!"

"Excuse me please!" Danvers broke in with some agitation. "That was T. S. Elliot and the final lines of the *Four Quartets*, wasn't it? But the last line is surely: *And the fire and the rose are one.*"

"No matter," Middlesex replied unabashed. "Of all the flowers, the rose is the most mysterious – of innocence and virginity; of resurrection and faction; of pleasure and delight. So of all creatures, the Green Rabbit is the most mysterious, linking 'time past with time future, through time present.'"

"Elliot again!" Danvers cried.

"Quite, quite," Sir Magnus nodded wisely. "I believe we did him last month," he added, remembering Danvers' eulogy about the poet on a drive up to London. He was as deeply engrossed in the Open University Course as his chauffeur, who was studying for a degree at his expense.

"I don't know who this Elliot person is," Sergei broke in, "but does he write everything in capitals, Middlesex? Or how did you come to read him?"

"No, no," Middlesex replied. "You see, while I was down in the West Country, I attended a poetry reading, and I was most impressed. He was buried at East Coker – the village from which his family emigrated to the States in the seventeenth century."

"May one ask what you were doing in the West Country?" the Captain asked.

"Had it anything to do with the Quest, you being there?" Dasha asked.

Middlesex picked up a large plate of salad. "Indeed it had! I remembered your remarks about 'lay lines', Mr Danvers, and I followed them as closely as I could to Glastonbury."

"And.. ?" Dasha was impatient.

Middlesex chewed thoughtfully on a lettuce leaf. "And I found and circumnavigated all the signs of the Zodiac, which are carved into the fields and the landscape. It was most fascinating!"

"But did they lead you any nearer to the answers to your own questions?" Mrs Polenski wanted to know.

"No, not directly," Middlesex answered slowly. "But while I was in that area, I heard tell of some interesting carvings."

"Where did you stay?" Dasha demanded suddenly, at a tangent.

Middlesex was nonchalant. "Here…and there."

"But did you find another family?" her anxious tone betrayed her jealousy.

"You are my family," Middlesex replied simply, "With your permission, that is," was added with irresistible charm and directly at the Captain and Mrs Polenski.

"Do we have any choice in the matter?" the Captain asked, laughing.

"Stop it, Dad," Sergei said unexpectedly. "You know none of us want any choice. Middlesex adopted us – and that's how it should be."

"Well said, young man!" Sir Magnus applauded him. "But let us return to the carvings. They were in churches, I presume?"

Middlesex nodded. "Around the area of Dartmoor, in Widdicombe Church in particular, I found carved motifs almost identical to the one in your new room, Captain."

"Did you find out what they are?" asked Mrs Polenski.

"They are called Tinner's Rabbits, Mrs Mum. Three large rabbits obviously of Green Aristocratic vintage like myself – chasing each other in circular pattern."

"What are tinners?" Dasha asked, voicing the universal ignorance.

"As the name implies, they are workers of the metal tin," Middlesex explained. "Tin has been mined in Cornwall for thousands of years, you know. The Phoenicians are the first known traders, but whether it was they who introduced the Green Rabbit to these islands, or whether they took my ancestors from here to the lands of the Mediterranean is, and will no doubt remain, a moot point."

"You've lost me," the Captain confessed. "How do you know that the civilizations of the Mediterranean knew anything about your lot?"

Middlesex looked smug, as he sipped the chilled cabbage juice thoughtfully supplied by Sir Magnus. "During the course of my researches, I have come across pictorial representations of Green Rabbits in hunting scenes from Egypt of the New Kingdom around 1500 BC, on a vase from ancient Greece and on a Roman knife."

"Honestly!" Dasha was dazzled by Middlesex erudition. "Anything more?"

Middlesex nodded. "We are seen in hieroglyphs on a coffin in Thebes from the twenty-first dynasty along with a picture of a divinity which has a Green Rabbit head. My ancestry is longer, and even more distinguished, than I had imagined."

There was a long pause as each digested this potted history of *Lapidus Aristocratua*, along with sherry trifle and cakes. It was Sergei who, being the fastest eater, set the conversation off again. "Then how do you explain that rabbit thing being in our house. They didn't mine tin round here, did they?"

Middlesex delicately wiped green whiskers free of celery. "Obviously there were tinners, otherwise known as white smiths, in places far away from the mines. Tin is used in many alloys – especially with copper to make bronze."

"I still don't see what that has to do with here," Sergei persisted.

"Well, I'm sure that when we have looked properly at the books in the hidey-hole, we shall find the connection," Middlesex said confidently. "In fact, although I have not been there yet, I understand there is a Tinner's Rabbits window as near here as Long Melford church."

Mrs Polenski jumped up and, with expertise of the trained researcher, went straight to White's Gazetteer for Suffolk, 1844. Turning to Long Melford, she found the evidence.

"Listen to this," she called out, "Among the tradespeople in 1844, there was William Downs, whitesmith; Thomas Parsonson, tinner; David Ward and James Silver – even his name is a give-away! – iron and brass founders. You're absolutely right, Middlesex."

"Thank you, Mrs Mum," Middlesex responded graciously. "But then G-R-I-L is infallible!"

"From my reading on the subject," Danvers attempted to prick the balloon of Middlesex's fancy, "I suspect that you may be confusing Green Rabbit with hares."

Middlesex laughed with delight. "Point taken, Mr Danvers. But you know, throughout history, from China and back again, your species has confused the rabbit and the hare. And we, *Lapidus Aristocratus*, are the link. We are the reality behind the universal myths, ranging from Brer Rabbit to the ancient Egyptian divinity."

"Are you using 'we' in the royal sense?" the Captain asked with amusement.

Middlesex nodded. "It would seem that, for the present, I am guilty of that because I have not yet found another of my kind."

"There may be a reason for our seeming confusion, Middlesex," Mrs Polenski said thoughtfully. "During our early history, you know, it was definitely Non-U to call the spirits and deities by their right names. Yes, you may be right that the myths and legends, attributed to hares, were in fact a cover-up for the true identity of the symbol of regeneration and fertility."

"I thought hares were supposed to be scatter-brained, cunning – and mad!" Sergei said innocently.

"That certainly strengthens Middlesex's case," his father laughed.

"Are you saying that you're a pagan god?" Dasha asked Middlesex, perplexed.

Her mother interrupted forcibly. "I have never liked that word 'pagan'. According to the dictionary, it means 'not Jewish, Christian or Muslim; in fact, an unenlightened person.' The arrogance of it."

"*Pagan – pagus,*" Sir Magnus recited, as wisps of long-forgotten Latin lessons floated back into memory. "*Pagus* means a country place and, of course, to the citizens of a great city-state like Rome, all non-city dwellers were bumpkins, *ipso facto!*"

"A misconception which still operates today, if I may say so," commented Danvers, the son of a farm labourer.

"This is Capital!" Middlesex cried. "Your arguments fortify G-R-I-L's contention: that my race was known and revered before the centralization of religion took place. That the new bureaucracies robbed us of our potency by deliberately confusing us with our near, but mundane, relatives."

"Quite, quite," Sir Magnus adjusted his monocle. "A slightly flippant example in our modern times, is the use of the Old Hundreds, now abandoned under re-organisation, as House names in schools."

The Captain laughed irreverently. "Civilization in a nutshell! Emulation to emasculation!"

Middlesex thumped the floor in delight with a green foot. "Capital, just splendid. That must be recorded in G-R-I-P!"

"Right then, let's have it. Green Rabbit Instant... ?" Sergei cried.

"Proverbs," Middlesex grinned. "Green Rabbit Instant Proverbs! What else?"

The warm, satiated silence enveloped them, broken only by the cracklings of logs. Cascades of sparks shot intermittently up the wide chimney, hypnotising drowsy eyes. Soon the only observer of the scene were the large, tranquil eyes of *Lapidus Aristocratus*.

Middlesex stood up hesitantly, then moved with caution towards the inviting gap in the wall. Taking a box of matches from the mantel shelf, the green presence moved noiselessly into the passageway. Once inside the tiny room, Middlesex lit the old candle, sat down on the high stool and surrendered to the spirit of the place. Contemplation drugged the senses and a green paw, of its own volition, stretched out to a large, grimy leather-bound book. With due reverence, it opened the book at the first page. There, ornate capital letters drew Middlesex's gaze and Itself began to read in a low whisper:

AN ACCOUNT OF YE DWELLING WORLD'S END ERECTED IN THE 28TH YEAR OF OUR SOVEREIGN LORD HENRY SIX ONE THOUSAND FOUR HUNDRED FIFTY ANNO DOMINI BY ADAM SMITH FREEMAN OF YE PARISH OF FARTHINGALE INFERIOR OF THE DESMESNE OF SIR RALPH DE VERTE.

Trembling with excitement, without knowing the cause, Middlesex turned the page. There, in colours as brilliant as the day they were painted, was the emblem of the Tinners' Rabbits, the three animals done with a vivid green pigment. Underneath was inscribed: THIS DAY, MARCH ONE HAS YE CONSECRATION BEEN MADE. KNOWE THAT NO SPRITE SPIRIT OR HOBGOBLIN SHALL EVER HOLD SWAY. WITH HEAD TO THE RISING OF THE SUN AND FEET TO THE SETTING BEING OF THE RIGHT GIRTH AND HUE THIS SACRIFICE BE MOSTE PROPITIOUS.

Middlesex shook with anticipation. The green glow intensified as G-R-A-S-S asserted its power and directed the dark eyes to the wall on the left. At its centre, Middlesex now discerned a break in the brickwork. Tentatively, green paws explored the wall and felt a length of wood, sanded and polished to a velvet finish. Carefully, the paws prised it from the wall, to discover that it was in fact an oak box fashioned in the shape of a tiny coffin. Laying the coffin on the bench, Middlesex sat down and breathed deeply to calm a racing heart. Then the lid was lifted. It was as G-R-A-S-S predicted it should be – the skeleton of a large rabbit lay with front paws crossed, and around its neck lay a silver chain bearing a small medallion. Exquisitely wrought in silver, it was again the Tinners' Rabbits motif.

Middlesex gazed at it in a state near to shock. Fingering the R.A.C. medallion, Middlesex understood for the first time why G-R-A-S-S had dictated that it be worn at all times. At last, the elastic of excitement snapped and Middlesex wanted to tell the others of the discoveries. At the end of the passage Middlesex paused briefly, to gaze round at the dark beams, pitted now with age, at the rise and fall of daub in the uneven walls, at the security bestowed on so many generations by Adam Smith and his sacrifice to the ancient faith.

"Wake up, everyone!" Middlesex shouted at last. "G-R-A-S-S has a great revelation to unfold to you."

Eyes opened. The twins remained in the limbo between dream and consciousness, but the adults quickly regained their faculties to the vague murmurings of *so sorry, I must have dozed off for a moment* and *it is very warm in here, isn't it?*

"It might be advisable for you to enter the room in couples," Middlesex said mysteriously. "If I might be so bold, I suggest that Dasha accompany the Captain, and Sergei with Mrs Mum. That leaves Mr Danvers to go with Sir Magnus."

Sir Magnus adjusted his eye-glass. "You have a natural talent for the dramatic, my dear friend," he remarked urbanely. "What is the order of precedence?"

Middlesex, appreciative of Sir Magnus' remark, rose to the occasion. "Family first, I think, would be in the best taste. Captain, you and Dasha perhaps.... ?"

"I hope your exhibits are worthy of this build-up," the Captain laughed as he led the way.

The others, trying to catch the gist of the exclamations and excited words that floated down the passageway, did not note Middlesex's departure.

Out in the clear chill of the October night, Middlesex breathed deeply. Green fur drank in energy from light that had been travelling since the world was new. G-R-A-S-S propelled green feet towards the Norman church flintily stolid and square; forbidding as the mailed fists of the Conqueror's men, until Middlesex stood immediately outside and below the altar window. The green glow dimly illuminated the plain glass window, ablaze now with the fire of Virginia Creeper that curtained the stony fretwork. Middlesex looked down at tile grass beneath and knew, though there was no stone or marker, that directly below lay whatever remained of Adam Smith, Freeman, who had known the secret of the Green Rabbit.

By the time Middlesex returned, the Rolls had departed and the cottage lay sleeping away another night in its long history. In the hall, a note written in capitals lay on the table. "YOUR ROOM IS READY. SLEEP WELL – AND THANK YOU. MRS MUM."

Middlesex smiled, but crept noiselessly into the lounge. Tonight, a chair facing the passage that would lead perhaps to self-realization, was bed enough.

CHAPTER XI

Mechanical power is but an expression of spiritual force
(B. O. P. Bk. 2)

Middlesex slept soundly, and late. Indeed it was the clatter from the kitchen that eventually bought Itself to consciousness in time to hear Dasha arguing: "But Middlesex must have gone, Mum. The bed has never even been touched."

"And it's Hallowe'en tonight," Sergei went on in grumbling tones. "I call it a really mean trick – just appearing like that, and then taking off without a word."

Middlesex, stiff from the limited space in the armchair, hurried to the half-open kitchen door and poked a green head round it, ears held at an ashamed angle and shouted: "Now you see me, now you don't!"

"Oh, Middlesex," Dasha cried in relief, running to the door, "you are a beast! Where have you been all night?"

"Me? I've been sleeping soundly, in the lounge!" Itself laughed, before turning to Mrs Polenski, the picture of contrition. "I hope you're not too annoyed with me, Mrs Mum. I was too... too exhilarated to go to my bed. I wanted to sleep where could see the passageway."

"I could pull your ears off!" Sergei shouted, still upset.

"You really thought I'd go and let you have all the fun tonight?" Middlesex retorted. "Not a chance, my friend, there is much to be done!"

"In that case, I'm going to take out insurance with Lloyds on my sanity," the Captain announced, as he strode into the kitchen. "I still can't believe that last night really happened."

"Dad, that's mean," Dasha admonished her father.

"Yes, dear," Mrs Polenski added in tones of reproval. "We all know how much it must have meant to Middlesex."

The Captain shrugged his shoulders and sat down. He had sense enough to recognise defeat when it glowered at him across the table. "I'm sorry," he said, "but actually I was referring to the black comedy in the early part of the evening."

"That was unfortunate," Middlesex conceded. "But I trust that you join with me, in the sentiment that, in this instance, the end more than justified the means."

"You're right, of course," the Captain admitted. "Nevertheless, as an Englishman by nature and nurture, though not by name, I claim my birth-right of a good grumble to relieve my soul."

"Splendid, capital!" Middlesex declared, attacking with enthusiasm the bowl of muesli, which Mrs Polenski bad just put out.

Over the toast and marmalade, Sergei started on a long series of questions which had been shooting through his mind all night. Between them Mrs Polenski and Middlesex explained that it had been an age-long custom to bury or enwall a sacrifice in a new building, to ward off evil spirits from the soil who might do the building mischief. Once, they said, it had been human sacrifices, even in Christian times as when St. Columba had buried St. Oran under his church on Iona. They went on to say that cats, because they were the "familiars" of witches, were often used, and their mummified bodies or skeletons had been found many times in cottages.

"But why a rabbit in this cottage?" Dasha protested. "They've got nothing to do with witches, have they?"

"On the contrary," her mother replied. "In many parts of the country, the local name for a hare is 'puss'. And we must remember, as Middlesex pointed out, rabbits and hares have been confused with each other all through the ages."

"Which is not so surprising," Middlesex added, "when one remembers that *Lepidua Ari. atocratus* was much larger than the 'bunny' rabbit. Of course, I think that I am exceptional – unique, in fact…"

"But of course!" the Captain mumbled.

"So you see," Mrs Polenski went on, ignoring her husband, "hares, green rabbits if you like, were also thought of as witches' familiars..."

"What I don't understand," Dasha said flatly, "is why some animals are thought of as being muddled up with witches in the first place."

"And what are witches anyway?" Sergei asked derisively. "It's a load of old nonsense..."

"If you think about the old civilizations, like Greece and Rome and Egypt," their mother began quietly, "you'll remember that they set great store by oracles and sooth-sayers, who talked with the gods and knew the future. And do you know what sex they were nearly always?"

"Women, I'll bet!" the Captain ventured, as interested as the twins.

"That's right, they were," his wife answered. "Then Christianity came along, and the early fathers decreed that it should be men only who contacted their god, and that to know or pretend to know the future was the work of the devil. So, the oracles and soothsayers, who were women anyway and therefore inferior, were demoted to being agents of the devil."

"And cats and hares – and Green Rabbits, where do they fit in?" Sergei wanted to know.

"They were divinities in their own right," replied his mother. "And so they had to be discredited too. The rumour was spread around that they were hand-in-glove with the new race of witches; that they were their help-meets, their familiars."

"But that doesn't make sense," Sergei protested. "You just said that they were buried in new buildings to protect them."

"Quite so," Middlesex agreed. "You see, the memories of the ancient gods lingered on in the popular mind as the so-called 'pagan' superstitions, and the less sophisticated often turned to them for protection and good fortune."

"True, true!" agreed the Captain, laughing. "Mistletoe and knock-on-wood, rolling eggs down a hill at Easter, the great feast of Saturnalia at the December equinox, the devil's cloven hoof straight from Pan! Pagan the whole lot of them!"

Further discussion was frustrated by the telephone bell. It was Sir Magnus. The Captain answered it and his side of the conversation consisted of: "Indeed it was... fascinating, extraordinary... yes, I'm sure they would... fine. In half an hour?... that's very kind of you."

"Well?" demanded Dasha as her father replaced the receiver thoughtfully.

"Well," the Captain hesitated and stared speculatively at Middlesex.

"Come on, Dad," Sergei begged impatiently. "What did Sir Magnus say?"

"You have been invited," the Captain said fatalistically, "on an outing with Sir Magnus. He has some business to attend to at Farthing Down Nurseries, and he thought... he thought you two and Middlesex might enjoy looking round the Railway Museum."

The Captain looked across at his wife. She shrugged, then said laughing: "Great Scot!"

"Precisely," said the Captain, "Great Scot."

"Great," Sergei shouted. "There won't be anyone else there."

"And where precisely is this 'there'?" Middlesex enquired.

"It's really a nursery and gardens, but the owner is a steam engine fanatic," the Captain explained. "He has a remarkable collection of traction engines, roundabouts and steam trains."

"And there is a railway line that goes right round the gardens," Dasha added with excitement.

"That'll be closed," said Sergei. "It's shut down for the winter."

"Not to worry," said Middlesex, and then added ominously: "I'm sure we'll find plenty of things to do."

Middlesex was enchanted. In the nursery fields, ranks of rotund chrysanthemums – bronze and white, yellow or dusky pink – preened themselves under autumn sun. Beyond a hedge, a bonfire smoked blue mist back over the fields as the debris of summer smouldered to white ash. By the lake self-conscious willows wept frail leaves onto water and grass, and ripe bulrushes stood sentinel beneath chocolate busbies.

Coot and moorhen fussed across the still water, neurotically busy among swans who sat the water like alabaster ornaments. Trees, some already filigree clean, others untidy with coloured leaves tenacious of life, etched prophetic messages on a blue sky. Among them, dark evergreens brooded; waiting the time, soon now, when they would be the luxuriant ones. Everywhere leaves, gaudy and brittle, spilled over grass and paths, as light and crunchy as potato crisps.

The twins were impatient to get to the engine sheds, but Middlesex was not to be hurried. At last, however, they came within sight of the traction engines, and Middlesex's mood underwent a transformation. With a loud cry of "Splendid, just Capital," Itself charged across the gravelled yard to where the great monsters stood.

Middlesex clambered up onto a driving platform, seized the driving wheel and embarked on an oratorio of *chug-chugs* that reverberated round the gardens. One of the Nursery staff appeared, having been forewarned by Sir Magnus about the unusual appearance of this visitor, and with instructions to humour any request – within reason!

"Does this really work?" Middlesex called out.

"It does... Sir," replied a startled Sam Pightle. "Would you like me to get up steam and take you all for a ride?"

"Oh yes, please," the twins shouted in unison.

"Mr Cutting has given his O.K." said Sam, "as long as I take you."

Middlesex glowed. "That is most kind of you – and Mr Cutting. It will be a great experience."

"It takes a bit of time to get the old lady ready," explained Sam, "so would you like to be looking round the loco. shed while you're waiting?"

Inside the loco. shed all of them were over-awed for some minutes by the sheer size and latent power of the engines. They felt dwarfed by the ruthless iron wheels, by the shining bars of the pistons and the crank-shafts.

"Aren't they enormous?" Dasha whispered, realizing, at ground level instead of platform level, the true size of a locomotive.

"I find it a little frightening," Danvers confessed. "I can't quite explain it, but they seem to sum up what the phrase 'Industrial Revolution' is all about..."

Middlesex hooted appreciatively. "A very clever play on words, Mr Danvers. But I do see what you mean. No wonder, then, that the Victorians had such an arrogant concept of their mastery of the world. To conceive and build such naked power. Truly remarkable!"

During this exchange, the twins had gone their own way.

"Hey Middlesex," they shouted, "come and see the Duke of Rutland. It says here that it's a Pacific Class 4-6-2 engine, whatever that means."

"Something to do with the wheel arrangement, I believe," Danvers said helpfully.

"But isn't it beautiful?" said Dasha.

Everything on the locomotive was painted black or gentian blue; the brass was highly polished and the pistons gleamed silver.

"And here's the Duchess of Rutland," Sergei shouted. "Atlantic Class 4-4-2. Weighs 14 tons; holds 44500 gallons of water and 7 tons of coal. Top speed 85 m.p.h."

The Duchess was robed in a green which vied with Middlesex. They went on to admire the Hibernian Pacific Class and the Celtic Flyer, sporting a four-leaved clover blazoned over its name.

"It says here," Sergei read out, "that it built up a pressure of 250 pounds to the square inch. Wow! And it wears a shamrock because it was on the London to Holyhead run for the Irish trade."

Middlesex was jumping on and off footplates like a yo-yo, ignoring the steps and doing it instead in one well-placed leap.

Levers, knobs, shovels, all came in for their fair share of attention as Itself provided live sound effects with force and flexibility.

As they made their way towards the door out of the shed, Middlesex's eye was drawn to a small engine standing by itself in the corner. It was a humble shunter, from the turn of the century. A 2-6-0 of the Mogul Class, read its ticket. The boiler was painted a dusky yellow, and all else a glossy black. The regulator valve of burnished copper was the shape of a hat-box. It had a narrow chimney, black, tall with a castellated rim. All the levers and controls were of brass, as was the name plate on the tender. Fortunately, it was in capitals: TREVITHICK.

"This is charming," Middlesex purred. "Quite perfect - a poem, in fact!"

Sergei snorted with disgust. "Cut it out, Middlesex. It's only a shunter, a maid-of-all-work. You really do get ucky at times."

"I am as I am," Middlesex retorted. "And I say this little engine is perfection. The line of it... the..."

"Oh, shut up!" Sergei shouted rudely.

Dasha came to the rescue. "What's the name on the side? Trevithick. I'm sure I've seen it somewhere before."

Middlesex ran a green paw over the embossed letters. "I can't say that I have, but it is certainly very unusual."

Danvers, who had just joined them was able to enlighten them. "Trevithick? Why that's the name of the man who built and used the first mobile steam engine. He was a mine owner in Cornwall, and he needed something to speed up the movement of the ore."

"There!" Middlesex was triumphant. "G-R-A-S-S recognised its uniqueness at once; saw the significance of its connection with..."

Sergei collapsed into laughter. "Do you pun here often? Honestly, Middlesex you'll be telling us next that the moon really is made of green cheese, which means it was made by a Green Rabbit, I suppose!"

"More than likely," Middlesex retorted, with mock seriousness. "The ancient Chinese even had a legend about the Hare in the Moon."

"And so do we," Dasha cried, joining in the fun "Listen:
Hey diddle, diddle,
The cat and the fiddle,
The hare jumped over the moon.
The brown bunnies laughed to see such fun,
When Middlesex played the buffoon!"

They all joined in a repeat rendering and applauded themselves heartily. Then, Middlesex jumping onto the Trevithick's footplate, announced in solemn tones: "Now, I am truly of the immortals. I have a nursery rhyme in my honour, conceived and written in a Nursery!"

"We must publish!" Danvers shouted. "Publish and be damned!" The door opened and Sam Pightle looked in apprehensively.

"She's all steamed up and ready to roll," he announced nervously.

"Capital, splendid!" Middlesex responded, leaping down from the footplate. "We are ready, sir."

They found Sir Magnus and Mr Cutting waiting by the steam engine. Sir Magnus introduced the twins, and then Middlesex. Itself held Mr Cutting's gaze and speaking softly said: "This marriage of the natural habitat and harnessed power was conceived by a 'green' imagination, Mr Cutting. I congratulate you," and yet another consciousness surrendered to the dark velvet secret of a Green Rabbit's eyes.

The twins took the first joy-ride up and down the field in The Queen Boadicea. Beneath the curved wooden roof, edged with a valence bearing her name and supported front and rear on twisting brass bars and cross-struts, the cylinder vibrated with a scorching power that coursed like greyhounds through her tubes. The front driving wheels with brass hub caps were dwarfed by the seven-footers at the rear. The vast, symmetrical chimney, ringed in brass, belched out black smoke while the muffled song of her exhaust – *mump, mump, mump, mump* – proclaimed that the Herculean strength was under control. Nervous at first, they soon learnt to trust the steady rhythm of her pistons. Then it was the turn of Sir Magnus and Middlesex and within minutes, G-R-I-L was at work, whispering that the principles of driving her were simple; all that was needed was a little practice. The twins pleaded for a second ride so, leaving Danvers with Middlesex and the twins, Sir Magnus sauntered back to the house with Jeremiah Cutting for some tiffin. As the twins and Middlesex had their second ride round the meadow with Sam Pightle at the wheel, many questions were prompted by G-R-I-L. The answers and demonstrations so innocently supplied by Sam, were filed away for future reference. When the ride was over, Sam told them that there was coffee and cakes for them up at the house, and that he had to go back to the greenhouses. It was as they started to walk back to the house that G-R-I-D swamped a Green mind and took command.

"I think that I'll walk round the lake again," Middlesex said, too casually.

Sergei winked at Dasha as he asked, "Mind if we come with you, Middlesex?"

"You would be most welcome," Middlesex replied blandly.

"I think I'll go on up to the house," Danvers said. "I could do with a cup of coffee," and hoping that something stronger might be on offer.

At last, the gardens were deserted; only the low, steady chug of the Queen broke the silence. The twins waited expectantly to see which way Middlesex would go, and they followed without comment when the expected happened. Middlesex bounded up onto the footplate of the Boadicea and shouted, "How about another jaunt around the meadow, you two? It's a shame to waste this head of steam."

Sergei laughed: "So that's it! I knew there was something up. But are you sure you know how to drive it?" He found the idea irresistible.

G-R-I-D as always endowed Middlesex with such overwhelming confidence, that a minute later Sergei and Dasha were on the footplate, being instructed by Middlesex on how and when to stoke the fire. Then Middlesex opened the throttle and the governor spun giddily. Middlesex released the brake lever and put her into first gear. The leviathan moved with slow majesty; crankshaft proclaiming strength in the smooth thunder of its movement. The Boadicea gained speed, the governor spinning like a giro top, as Middlesex took her up into second gear.

"I am the steersman of the Boadicea and a mighty Queen is she!" Middlesex shouted, allowing the speed to build up for top gear.

The twins were beginning to get anxious. "Slow her down, Middlesex," Sergei shouted. "You'll need to turn soon."

Middlesex, however, had not idea of turning, having previously noted that the driveway passed the top of the meadow.

"I must just see what she feels like on a smooth surface," came the ominous reply. "I'll bet she'll really roll then…"

"No, Middlesex, no!" Dasha protested, more as a matter of form than out of conviction that she could have any influence.

"But it's so bumpy, "Middlesex protested. "I won't go far - and you're quite safe! G-R-I-L assures me that we are all safe."

The twins gave up and, recalling the ride in the Rolls and Middlesex's exploits as a pilot, just hoped that Lady Luck was in a good mood today.

Middlesex throttled back; the little balls on the governor slowed down and, in a smooth curve the Queen Boadicea chugged onto the drive.

"Isn't this super?" Sergei shouted.

"It certainly is," Middlesex agreed smugly, stroking the brass controls with a loving paw. "Think how smooth it would be on the road then – and we could let her rip up into top gear."

"Oh. Middlesex, dare we?" Sergei said longingly. "But what about Dad and Mr Cutting… and Sir Magnus?"

"G-R-I-L will provide," Middlesex assured him happily. "And, in any case, G-R-A -S-S advises me that it is a necessary act."

The twins burst out laughing. "Oh, alright then," said Dasha fatalistically, "we're with you, but we must be mad, too!"

"One needs to be a little mad in order to retain one's sanity," Middlesex laughed back, as with a penetrating, "Whoops, here we go then!" green paws swung the wheel, and The Queen Boadicea swung out into the road.

Fortunately for all concerned, it was a byroad leading only to Farthing Down and a couple of other farms. The royal progress progressed smoothly as speed built up and the Queen achieved top gear. Intrepid explorers, the three of them gazed out over a familiar landscape with the wonder of an Eskimo taking a first glimpse of an equatorial jungle.

Middlesex kept a wary eye on the governor balls and dials, and negotiated small bends with consummate ease.

"We must be getting near to the T-Junction now," Sergei warned, recognising a small bridge as they rolled over it. "We'd better turn back because the other road is a very busy one."

To his relief, Middlesex agreed but then came the sting. "There is one small point. I don't know if there's a reverse gear - otherwise we shall have to circle round somewhere!" Middlesex confessed.

Before the twins had time to blow their tops, an incredible sight revealed itself as they rounded the last corner to the junction. Just beyond the turn to the left towards Westbury, a great sugar-beet lorry had skidded and turned somersault. It lay across the road with its load of knobbly sweetness scattered crazily in every direction. A milk tanker, coming from the opposite direction a moment later, had swerved, skidded and it, too, had landed on its side. Now its content s were pouring out, creating a white sea in the middle of which the two drivers, shaken but unhurt, were hurling abuse at each other. A red sports car, coming up too quickly behind the tanker, aquaplaned on the milk and spun round and ended up on the wrong side of the road facing in the wrong direction.

Even as Queen Boadicea stopped at the junction, the queue of cars from each direction was building up. Drivers got out to survey the disaster area; others used their horns in futile impatience, but nobody did anything constructive.

Then the Law arrived, with blue flashing lights and serge-blue efficiency. The sergeant from Westbury, unfortunately, noticed the Queen and recognised the green glow before he recognised the true state of affairs. Remembering P.C. Wimble's memo of the previous evening, he reached an erroneous, if understandable, conclusion. His blood pressure soared as, ignoring all else, he strode towards the Queen. His arrival coincided with that of Danvers in the Rolls, and Mr Cutting and Sir Magnus in a Range Rover. They had been alerted by Danvers who, getting anxious when the others had failed to join him at the house, had heard the sound of a traction engine revving up.

So as a combined raiding party advanced on the Queen, Middlesex waved a friendly paw and shouted cheerily: "It's like the Boston Tea Party – without the tea!"

A cacophony of voices bellowed an assortment of replies, but the sergeant shouted them all down. "You'll get ten years for this! I'll see to it personally. Do you realize I have the wife of the Chief Constable in a car back there about to give birth? How do you propose we get her to Westbury then?"

"Oh dear," Middlesex was all concern. "You *have* got a problem."

While the Sergeant sought for words to combat Middlesex's seeming impudence, Sir Magnus, who had been appraising the situation, said calmly: "My dear friend, I really fail to understand how you have managed to create this havoc."

"But we'd nothing to do with it," Sergei shouted loudly. "The accident had already happened when we got here!"

"What can I do?" the Sergeant shouted helplessly. "Can anyone here deliver a baby?"

"Danvers, would you come here please?" Sir Magnus called genially.

"Oh no, Sir Magnus, begging your pardon," Danvers said formally, backing away, "Midwifery is not in my syllabus, or in my contract!"

"Don't panic, man," Sir Magnus replied, unruffled. "Our problem lies in obtaining, quickly, suitable tackle to move the lorry and the tanker, in order that the car carrying the little mother-to-be can get through. I want your ideas as to the best course of action."

"There's no problem," Middlesex shouted airily, embracing the pulsating Queen in a magnificent sweep of a green arm. "We have here the ultimate in lifting gear. Now, if you gentlemen would assist me?"

"Middlesex, you're a genius," Sergei shouted.

Middlesex turned and laid green paw aside green nostrils. "G-R-I-L and G-R-A-S-S are an infallible combination!" Itself crowed with a triumphant laugh.

Within minutes, the Queen was moved into position and her massive towing chains had been attached to the lorry.

Middlesex paused for a moment, heightening the effect and then, with a mighty yell of "Anchors away!" opened the queen's throttle to maximum and gave the lowpress cylinder the 'gun'. To cheering and horned applause, the beet lorry was moved to one side as easily as a child moves a toy lorry. With so many willing hands, the chains were quickly transferred to the milk tanker, and that was soon deposited on the other verge, to even more tumultuous applause. Then the Sergeant posted a man at each end of the White Sea before returning to his patrol car. Using extreme caution, the driver skimmed over the milky road, followed by the Chief Constable's car. As it was the Chief's first experience of expectant fatherhood, he was in a state of greater agitation than his wife, who waved happily to Middlesex and the cheering motorists as she passed slowly by.

"Splendid! Just capital!" Middlesex exclaimed happily. "What a day! I feel positively exhilarated."

"How do you do it, Middlesex?" Sergei moaned. "How is it that you always end up the hero when you've done something outrageous?"

Middlesex beamed smugly. "Just let H-I-L and H-A-S-S guide you - and you, too, can be like me!"

"H-I-L and H-A-S-S? Whatever are they?" Dasha asked puzzled.

"Can't you guess? Human Instant Logic and... Human Automatic Sixth Sense!" the twins shouted, laughing. "I bet it doesn't work in the same way for us," Sergei added pensively. "But I'm going to give it a try, all the same..."

"I think we're going to need it right now!" Dasha said, as Sir Magnus and Danvers clambered up onto the footplate. The baronet's expensive tweed suit and fur-lined coat were very much the worse for wear, and Danver's smart uniform too was bespattered by the blizzard of milk which the cars had sprayed up as they got under way again.

"That was a magnificent show, dear friend," Sir Magnus said warmly. "I think even old Jeremiah is willing to forgive the liberty you took with his prize exhibit..."

"Whatever made you do it?" Danvers asked.

"It was my responsibility entirely," Middlesex claimed. "G-R-I-L and G-R-A-S-S insisted, although," Itself hesitated briefly, "although to be honest, the initial suggestion did come from G-R-I-D!"

"And to be even more honest, I think there was also a bit of H-I-D in it," Sergei owned up.

"And what will H-I-D be then?" Danvers asked dubiously.

Middlesex winked. "Human Instant Desire. But thank you, Sergei, for talking a share of the blame, but I think I must accept full responsibility. I shall offer my sincere apologies to Mr Cutting."

A few minutes later, the fire engine and breakdown vehicles arrived from Westbury. The road was hosed down and the offending vehicles were towed away. With things more or less back to normal, the little cavalcade returned to Farthing Down in reverse order. The Range Rover, whose driver was assuring Sir Magnus that as things had turned out such an incident, and its inevitable publicity, would attract both volunteers and money to his society for The Preservation of Steam Engines; the Rolls, whose driver was experiencing pangs of envy at Green Rabbit panache; and the Boadicea, whose driver was euphoric, and was bellowing, in unison with the twins, their private version of *Hey Diddle Diddle*.

When Sir Magnus returned the twins and Middlesex back home an hour later, a very puzzled Captain and Mrs Polenski greeted them. There had been a phone call, from the Maternity wing at Westbury General Hospital from the Sergeant to say that it was a girl; that mother and baby were both fine.

"Splendid, just Capital!" Middlesex crowed. "How's that for timing?"

"Excellent!" Sir Magnus congratulated his friend. "But you must excuse me, dear friends, I have a ghost or two to attend to for tonight. I'll see you around eight, I trust."

As the Rolls purred up the lane, Middlesex and the twins unfolded the morning's saga to the Captain and his wife.

"So, you see, Dad, "Sergei rounded off the tale, "I think we... I mean Middlesex and the Boadicea saved the Sergeant's bacon with his Chief. I bet he's our friend for life!"

"Incredible," the Captain murmured. "It's simply incredible!"

Mrs Polenski's reaction was more pragmatic. "I do hope," she said, as she went to make a cup of tea, "that the Chief doesn't call his baby daughter Boadicea in honour of the rescue!"

They all laughed as Sergei said, "She'll be a right little spitfire if they do. Honestly, Dad, riding on one of those engines is like... it's like..."

"Like riding a thunder bolt?" his father suggested.

"Right!" Dasha agreed. "Just like riding a thunder bolt!"

CHAPTER XII

Parts combine to make the whole; but that is not reality
(B. O. P. Bk. 3)

Sir Magnus was replete. The remains of his euphemistically labelled 'Ploughman's Lunch' littered the table - homemade bread from stoneground flour; the cheeses of Stilton, Gruyere and Denmark; butter from the Home Farm; and mead brewed to a recipe from the Abbey in Bury St. Edmunds. Logs danced their way to flaming death, and music spilled softly from quadraphonic speakers. Sir Magnus drew deeply on his cigar and congratulated himself on choosing a light repast in preparation for the evenings extravagances. He also congratulated himself that his little gamble had paid off. The gilt-edged invitations, which had been sent out the previous week, were in Middlesex's name as well as his own, with the enigmatic R.A.C. emblazoned at the top. He chuckled softly, imagining their reception in certain establishments.

The Reverend Eustace Pilke was also replete, on sausage and chips, in the austere dining room at the Rectory. He moved his angular frame into the worn comfort of a leather armchair; long legs fidgeting, even at rest, vainly seeking a clerical posture. Oblivious to the chirping of his long-suffering wife, he meditated on his sense of unease. While Sir Magnus was a generous patron of the Church, and the Lady Beatrice an enthusiastic member of the congregation on her rare visits home, the events of Midsummer Eve still teased his dreary mind. A mind which now sought to insure human souls as once, as an insurance salesman, it had sought to insure their bodies. Now it probed the propriety of this green apparition, which had mesmerised his village on Midsummer Eve, and now summoned him to Hallowe'en revelries. Witches and ghoulies; warlocks and spirits - and things that go bang in the night! Midsummer and Hallowe'en, he pondered; so many pagan undertones. The Reverend Pilke was worried. Perhaps it would be as well if he were there - just in case!

"Here, try it on, dear!" It wasn't his wife's voice so much as the feel of a strange object on his head that brought him back.

"Whatever are you doing, Anthea?" he demanded irritably.

"Trying on your hat for tonight, dear," his wife answered, soothing.

The Reverend moved it from his head and gazed in horror at the star and moon-spangled wizard's hat.

"My dear Anthea, have you taken leave of your senses?"

"But Eustace, it's so pretty!" Anthea mumbled.

"And so pagan!" he shot back angrily.

"Then what will you wear?" she asked, crestfallen, unable as usual to guess the source of her husband's displeasure.

The Reverend regarded the hat solemnly, and the answer descended.

"I shall remove the stars and spangles, like this... take away the brim, so... and what do you have now?"

"I don't know dear, what do you have?"

The Reverend Pilke was triumphant. "You have, my dear Anthea, a Grand Inquisitors hat, and what could be more appropriate than that!"

"If you say so dear, I'm sure it will be most appropriate," his wife agreed dutifully.

"I do so say, indeed. The Reverend Pilke suddenly regained his composure. "You are a good wife, Anthea. You may kiss me."

But no such marital harmony existed in the Crumble's dining room.

"It was a very fresh piece of fish I got you," Martha observed conversationally, as she attacked her hamburgers and chips.

Fred belched discreetly, and felt a sudden hatred for the white milk sea and its emasculated inhabitant, awaiting final consummation, on the plate before him.

"I do think you might limit eating chips to the occasions when I am not here," he grumbled. "You know how much I like them!"

Martha's quick temper flared. "I'll eat in the kitchen then," she snapped, and swept plate, cutlery and her outraged soul out of the room.

Fred sighed, took a mouthful of fish, and returned to the horns of his dilemma. Was he invited to Farthingale Hall to report or to socialize? The fact that Martha was included indicated a social role.

On the other hand, the re-emergence of this green creature kindled doubts in a probing mind which, until Martha's ambition and his editorial ulcers, had made him a first class reporter. Now, a square peg locked in a round hole, he employed his fertile imagination to create, out of Sir Magnus, a newspaper tycoon in the Hearst tradition. Should one of his master's whims be misinterpreted, and Fred Crumble was convinced that he would be discarded like a spent light bulb.

The lightly steamed haddock slipped down unnoticed into a stomach clenched in indecision. He hardly registered the removal of his empty plate and the substitution of an anaemic junket, so obsessed was he by the necessity to make the 'right' decision.

"Which hat are you planning to wear, then?" Martha asked from the opposite end of the table, her outburst over. Her temper rose and fell, obedient to her whim, as a gas flame to the turn of the tap.

Fred toyed with his spoon. "I don't know... I haven't made up my mind, but I do know that I ought to take a camera!"

"Whatever for?" Martha delicately wiped some cream from the corner of her mouth. "I thought we were going to a party."

"Yes, I know," Fred agreed unhappily. "But it's this Middlesex thing, you see. Does Sir Magnus want publicity or not?"

"For goodness sake! It's only one of his practical jokes. You know what he's like!"

"Yes I know, but then on the other hand, I don't know."

Martha Crumble regarded her husband impatiently. "I'll take the Instamatic in my handbag. But I don't think our lord and master will want his private party all over the front page. Now does that satisfy you?"

Fred pushed his junket away, untouched. "It's all so difficult. One wrong decision and I'll be on the breadline!"

Fred's ulcers were having a field day and he winced, but out of the pain came inspiration. "I've got the solution," he crowed. "I'll go as a film director. Large dark glasses and a beret!"

"And how will that help?" asked a sceptical Martha.

"Then I can legitimately wear a large camera... even take my flash."

"Just so long as you know what you're doing," was all Martha would say as she began to clear the table.

"I would not have not reached the position I have," Fred retorted testily, "if I didn't know what I was doing!"

He reached for his junket and demolished it in three mouthfuls.

"Now, I'm going into town for the glasses and beret. Are you coming?"

The twins were also in town with their father. They ordered flowers for the new baby and her mother, before going on to their favourite junk stall on the market for bits and pieces for their hats and masks for the party.

Middlesex stayed at WORLD'S END to help with the washing up, and to concoct a suitable hat.

"Have you found any of your answers yet?" Mrs Polenski asked conversationally, hands deep in the soap suds.

Middlesex sighed. "It is very strange, Mrs Mum. G-R-I-L and G-R-A-S-S have led me to many places; directed me to many vital clues. But my identity, I now perceive, does not lie in plurality."

Mrs Polenski rubbed hard on a clean plate: "I don't think I'm quite with you," she confessed.

Middlesex laughed. "Nor I with me! You see, I have found many answers but not THE answer, and that is all that is of any significance."

"But perhaps if you tried to put the answers you have together..." Mrs Mum suggested helpfully.

"No, no! Mrs Mum ," Middlesex was excited. "The truth of myself is not a jigsaw. G-R-A-S-S knows, and G-R-I-L insists that it is not so!"

"But all these leads, all these clues? All this evidence of the long history of your species?" Mrs Mum persisted.

Middlesex, absent-mindedly wiping an already dry plate, gazed out of the window at some late chrysanthemums. "Those flowers, Mrs Mum, they too have a long history. To comprehend them we can study them, dissect them, analyse the function of each part and its inter-relation with the whole; we can name each part and each part of each part. We can trace their evolution from the first amino acid; we can consider their emotional significance in cultures of differing place and time. But that does not give us the chrysanthemum. We have only comprehended it, but its identity eludes us."

Mrs Polenski turned and looked into the dark, velvet eyes. "Then what is it that you seek, Middlesex?" she asked softly.

"G-R-I-L directs and G-R-A-S-S dictates," Middlesex replied with authority, "that to comprehend is but to understand much, and know little."

"But I still don't follow you. If you fit the parts together, surely..."

"No, Mrs Mum, no, no! I, like you, comprehend too much of the trivial; but apprehend nothing of the answer yet. But I do know that it does not lie in completing a jigsaw - and that, I suppose, is a kind of wisdom."

Mrs Polenski forgot the dishes, opened the kitchen door and walked out into the garden. Middlesex followed, tea-cloth in paw. She stopped by the bronze chrysanthemums and gently stroked the curled petals.

"But I do apprehend them, Middlesex, in all their autumnal beauty and glory."

"But consider - in a black infinity of space," Middlesex spoke softly, hypnotically, "without time or season; without context or comparison; without texture or colour; without love or comfort ; would it suffice, Mrs Mum, would that one flower be enough?"

The dark ripple of Itself's voice obliterated the garden, dissolved the world and the sun itself. Non-being swirled through her in an empty universe - and the chrysanthemum too dissolved. It was not enough.

Slowly, her being regathered into the familiar sunlight of a known place.

"No, Middlesex," she whispered, "it was not enough."

"Nor is it yet for me," Middlesex confessed. "Yet the answer to all quests lies beyond the point at which it is enough."

Suddenly, Mrs Polenski shivered. "We're getting in a bit too deep for me," she said with forced gaiety. "It all smacks a bit too much of 'see Naples and die'."

"In order to die, one must first be alive," laughed Middlesex. "And you have a lot of living to do yet, Mrs Mum, as well as a lot of washing up!"

Mrs Polenski laughed too and returned to the kitchen sink, and to conversation that flowed easily between them, but in a lighter vein. Only when she was putting the last plate in the cupboard, did she return to that deeper moment.

"You know, Middlesex, when you first came here in the summer, I wanted to analyse you, to comprehend you, to pin you down."

"I know, Mrs Mum, I know," Middlesex said tenderly. "And I appreciated your concern for me."

She smiled into the dark eyes contritely; "But I was on the wrong tack, wasn't I? What is needed is that we apprehend you, right?"

Middlesex nodded. "Right, Mrs Mum. We make our journey together - you and I, your wonderful family, Danvers and Sir Magnus."

The last name galvanized Mrs Polenski. "The party!" she exclaimed. "And my hat and mask are nowhere near ready. I do hope the children won't be too long," she called as she went up the stairs.

Middlesex wandered into the lounge, through the opening behind the bookcase and into the hidey-hole. Taking the small coffin from the niche, Itself sat down on the bench, looked up at the Tinners's Rabbits and surrendered to the spirit of that place.

CHAPTER XIII

Bats in the belfry are a natural phenomenon
(B. O. P. Bk. 1)

Cold stars glittered coldly in a cold sky. A full moon reflected cold light over the frost-expectant landscape; a monochrome landscape of blacks and greys where all colour lay in the imagination. Over low fields, near water, white mist laid a fairy carpet over the too-solid earth creating a fit habitat for the sprites and spirits of ancient minds. Even the twins were silent as the Captain drove the old estate car slowly along the twisting lanes that led to Farthingale Hall. The wrought-iron gates were open, and large white arrows directed them to an improvised car-park. All Hallow's Eve - Sir Magnus style - had begun.

They were already in a mood to be startled when a fluorescent skeleton appeared at the car door and requested them to don warm black cloaks, and then to follow it. They came back to the main driveway on foot, to find that a mechanized broomstick awaited them. An estate lorry had been encased in the handles of a giant broomstick; the bristles of which towered over the driver's cab. Seats had been installed, and the Polenskis joined some of the other guests. Then the lorry, with its lights out, set off at a funeral pace up the quarter-mile drive.

Hollowed out mangolds swung from the trees, candle-light gleaming malevolently through crude eyes and mouths. Skeletons dangled from branches, and dark spectres with green eyes loomed through the trunks of ancient trees. Low and penetrating, moans and screams wailed balefully from hidden speakers, and echoed in the still air. And everywhere, animated, fluorescent skeletons danced grotesque contortions over the crackling grass.

Such was the success of Sir Magnus' stage management that there was a universal scream when a real, live owl swooped down, immediately in front of the lorry.

"Splendid, just Capital!" Middlesex hooted, flinging wide the great cloak and adding an eerie green glow to this unnatural world which enveloped them. Dasha had found her father's hand early on, and Sergei kept close by his mother.

As the lorry crawled round the circular path outside the great oaken doors of the Hall, Sir Magnus, who was waiting in the porch, opened the first bag of bats which his game-keepers had spent the day collecting in shed and barn. They flitted nervously upwards, only to turn and dart down again, their tiny radar squeaks piercing the moon-chilled air.

"Middlesex, my dear friend, " Sir Magnus called genially. "Come, you must help me receive our guests."

The oaken doors swung open, and the joint hosts took up their positions under the mellow light of a hundred candles in the great candelabra which illuminated the Great Hall. Only then was the magnificence of Sir Magnus' hat revealed. Fully a metre tall, it shimmered with jewelled stars, moons and a spiral of zodiacal signs that floated on a taut bed of royal-blue, silk damask. His monocle abandoned, the gentian eyes peered through a mask edged with silver braid. Middlesex adjusted a hat more modest but no less effective. One of Mrs Polenski's discarded black underslips was drawn tight over a card cone. Over it were scattered Tinners' Rabbits laboriously drawn and cut out of foil by the twins and Middlesex. As a mask had been found to look absurd worn over a furry green face, they had made one out of stiff card and attached it to the ebony stick. This was held foppishly in one paw, and was raised at each new encounter. Middlesex had practised the movement before a mirror until it had become a poem in action.

Mulled punch, pungent and spicy, awaited the guests, and was ladled out of the enormous Regency tureen by Marley's ghost, alias Mr Tubble of the Green Man. Even Sergei and Dasha were allowed small doses, but found that it made them sneeze. As the last arrivals made for the punch bowl, Sir Magnus beckoned to Middlesex to follow him up the wide stairs to the Musicians Gallery; sadly now only accommodating the modern trickery of a music centre and young Tubble as Master of the Knight's Musick.

"The old place approves of this gathering," Sir Magnus commented happily. "Can't you feel the old timbers stirring, the old heart-beat quickening? Look at the panels preening themselves in the candle glow; at the windows sparkling with old reflections."

Middlesex nodded. "*Time past and time future are all perhaps contained in time present!* said the poet. You have a great gift, Sir Magnus. Tonight you are creating eternity!" Middlesex sipped at the chilled cabbage juice, thoughtfully supplied by Banquo's ghost, alias Kemp the tractor driver, and asked: "Was it on a whim, or a stroke of genius, Sir Magnus, that you requested hats and masks with modern dress?"

"Just my appetite for variety, dear friend," Sir Magnus replied. "We had fancy dress last time, if you recall." He leaned over the balustrade and reconsidered. "On the other hand it is remarkably effective. After all, it is what is worn on the head, or at least it was what was worn on the head that denoted one's station and function in life - or our unadorned species, that is."

"Very true," Middlesex agreed. "But I am not unadorned, and my ears indicate my inner state of well-being, not my social role."

"But then my species," Sir Magnus laughed, "have always paid more attention to the outward show than to the inner grace."

"And what of the hatless world of today?" Middlesex parried.

"I think we've gone back to square one," chuckled Sir Magnus. "It's hair now, not hats, that communicate the message as to how one wishes the world to see one."

"Perhaps it is a new beginning," said Middlesex optimistically. "Perhaps your species will find, at long last, its identity - and the one flower will be enough."

"Quite, quite!" Sir Magnus assented vaguely. "Ah, here are your young friends."

The twins had discovered bob-apple in the morning room, and they were determined that Middlesex should join in the fun. But there was no contest, as they quickly discovered for Middlesex, exploiting the two long rodent teeth, caught the apple at first stab every time. To even things up a bit, Sergei then insisted that

Middlesex should be blindfolded, but it was to little avail against G-R-A-S-S, and ghostly hands were kept busy replenishing the line of rosy apples. The twins took solace in the fact that their hands were much defter than green paws at shelling the roasted nuts from the log fire in the Hall.

There was Country and Western music in the withdrawing room for the 'youngs'; folksy dancing in the Long Gallery for the cultured; Gilbert and Sullivan softly laced with The Merry Widow in the Great Hall for the conventional. Young Tubble worked hard spinning the discs, making appropriate comments on each of the independent audio systems and knew the meaning of power. And through it all the 'dead' waited on the living, as Sir Magnus' spectral staff anticipated and fulfilled every need of Witch Doctor or Beau Geste; Chinese Empress or Bat Girl, or the Grand Inquisitor, alias the Reverend Pilke. Then as the grand-father of all grandfather clocks struck the ninth hour in the Great Hall, Sir Magnus walked down the stairs from the gallery. He beckoned the Mighty Wizard of Oz, alias Danvers of the Open University, to his side and together they called for silence.

"My friends," Sir Magnus began in his well-modulated voice, "I know that for most of you, this is your first visit to Farthingale Hall. This building was completed in 1558 but there are a few features, an odd beam or a section of floor, which has survived from the previous building. That house, according to family documents, was started in 1069 by the de Verte who came over with the Conqueror. However, instead of a guided tour, the wise Wizard of Oz has suggested a ghost hunt, which should take you painlessly to all parts of the building."

"Are there really ghosts here?" Sergei whispered to Middlesex.

"Without being offensive, Sir Magnus," The Grand Inquisitor boomed out, in melancholy tones, "is this not rather upsetting for the ladies... and for our young friends?"

"Speaking for myself," Mrs Polenski broke in sweetly, "I am no more nervous than you are, Rector."

"There is nothing to fear in this house," Middlesex added firmly. "G-R-A-S-S has tested the vibrations and they are good - very good!"

"Really!" the Grand Inquisitor was outraged. "I feel that as good Christians we should not tamper with..."

"Oh, stuff and nonsense, Eustace!"

Every head turned to stare at an Anthea with cheeks glowing and discreet subservience drowned in four cups of spicy punch. "It's only a bit of fun. I'm dying to explore every nook and cranny - I've wanted to for years and years."

"Anthea! Would you please allow me to decide in your best interest," hissed the Inquisitor. "I am, after all, experienced in matters spiritual."

Dasha, however, chose to save Anthea's Dutch courage being put to further test. "What do we have to do, Sir Magnus? And how can we prove that we've seen a ghost?"

"The Wizard of Oz has thought of everything, I assure you," Sir Magnus laughed. "And I do assure you, Rector, that all the ghosts at Farthingale Hall are benign - indeed all my ancestors were good patrons of your church!"

In the awkward pause that followed, the Wizard of Oz began to explain that a red tape adorned with white arrows had been laid down as guide- line along stairs and passages to take them on a circular tour of the Hall. They were free to explore all rooms, cupboards, chests and niches along the route in their own way and in their own time.

"But what about the ghosts?" Sergei demanded.

"If you should meet one," Sir Magnus smiled, "I am sure that he or she will give you a message, so unique, that it will be proof in itself."

"There, dear," soothed the unnaturally ebullient Anthea Pilke to her husband. "It's all a joke really," and, taking his reluctant hand, guided him after her, Grand Inquisitor's hat and all.

Film director Crumble took his wife on one side and whispered, "You've got the Instamatic in your bag, haven't you? It may be quicker in certain situations to use it."

Martha giggled, punch-happy, "You can't photograph a ghost!" but she checked her bag all the same. Then they followed in the footsteps of the Rector.

Next to go were the Captain and his wife, concealing their mutual misgivings at Middlesex being given the run of the place. Mr Cutting wanted to see the conservatories where lived some rare and exotic plants, so Susan Cutting tagged along with the Polenskis.

As the various groups drifted up the stairs, Middlesex announced to the twins that they would do the tour in the reverse direction, thus avoiding the crush! So at the top of the staircase, they turned right instead of left. Discreet lighting deepened the mellowed tones of oak panelling and polished floors where they walked slowly along, gazing at the family portraits. Dasha paused to look at the pensive Lady Arabelle de Verte, a simple, girlish face trapped in the excesses of Restoration extravagance. She read the plaque beneath: "*Arabelle, 4th wife of Sir Richard de Verte, mother to Rupert and Sara. 1650 – 1668.* Gosh, look, Middlesex, she was only eighteen when she died. I bet she died when her second baby was born." They went on to look at the next portrait. "It's him!" Dasha cried, resentful of the arrogance in eyes that stared at her over a gap of three centuries. "Sir Richard de Verte, 10th Baronet. 1604 – 1680." She did a rapid calculation. "He must have been over sixty when he married Arabelle. No wonder she looks so sad!"

"Oh come on, you're being soppy," Sergei urged them. "Let's try this room."

They swung open a heavy, studded door and crept in to what appeared to be an office. There were three large tables, with round carved Tudor legs, incongruously littered with filing trays, typewriters, a dictaphone, heat copier and telephones. Four ironbound coffers lined the walls, bearing their quota of twentieth century office equipment. On the walls were maps, ancient and modern, of Farthingale and the lands owned by the manor.

"This must be the counting house," said Middlesex. "Yes, look at the great lock on the door and..." Green paws pulled open the shutters, "and bars at the windows."

"So this is what a counting house is!" Dasha murmured. *"The king was in his counting house, counting out his money!"*

"Yes, this is where it all happened!" Middlesex explained. "On quarter-days, the tenants paid their rents and taxes; fines were levied, retainers hired and fired or paid their annual pittance - and afterwards my lord counted his often ill-gotten gains."

"I don't like this room," Dasha announced suddenly. "It gives me the creeps!"

"You have a sensitive heart," Middlesex said softly. "But you are right. This room, over the centuries has known much misery; much injustice!" They left the room and closed the door behind them in sombre mood.

They walked on, glancing briefly at de Verte children arrayed in clothes calculated to dismiss the myth of childhood. Then they came to a small embrasure with a mullioned window, through which the frosty moonlight filtered. Under the deep sill were a pair of curiously carved folded hands. Dasha ran her fingers over them.

"Aren't they strange?" she said. "I wonder what they're for?"

"I remember seeing hands sticking out of walls in a film on the telly," Sergei informed them. "And when you pressed them, a piece of the wall, that was really a door, opened."

Dasha laughed. "Let's see then," and she pressed down hard.

Before their incredulous eyes, a panel on one side of the embrasure slid back, to reveal a narrow flight of stairs.

"Ah! Splendid, capital!" Middlesex chuckled. "This shows promise!"

With the green glow to protect and guide them, the twins were only too happy to follow. There were only three steps up, and then it levelled out into a narrow passageway. Middlesex crept forward, drawn by some pin-points of light about two metres ahead.. When they reached them, they discovered that they were, in fact, tiny peep-holes drilled through the panelling of the room on the other side of the wall. They each found a hole to peer through and discovered that a whole bedroom was revealed to their gaze.

Sergei giggled. "It's just like one of those 'What the Butler Saw' at an amusement arcade. I wish someone would come in!"

"Somewhere along the line," Middlesex commented drily, "there must have been a very jealous and mistrusting lord of this manor."

"Ssh! there's someone coming," Dasha whispered.

Breathlessly, they watched the bedroom door open hesitantly, and then the Reverend Pilke and Anthea entered. The Reverend stood in the grip of a great *ennui*, but his wife darted round the room like a gad-fly. She admired the four-poster bed and its silken hangings, and then tried its modern interior-sprung mattress. Next she lifted the lid of the wonderfully carved linen chest, and was delighted when it opened out into a modern dressing table. Eventually she walked across to the wall with the peep-holes in it, and stared at it intently. Sergei and Dasha ducked, convinced that she must have seen their staring eyes, but Middlesex only winked at them and whispered. "Listen!"

"Eustace, just come and look at this tapestry," they heard her say, and then realized that they were staring through a tapestry-hung wall.

"Just come and look!" Anthea insisted with excitement. "It's got all the signs of the zodiac worked into it. Look, there's the bull... and the fish... and oh! look at the twins, they're like little cherubs!"

"You will please come with me, Anthea," her husband replied coldly. "I have had enough of this..."

But his sentence remained unfinished, as a penetrating keening suddenly flooded the room with eerie insistence.

Anthea dashed into the arms of her protector and, for once, he did not rebuff her.

"I can see you," Middlesex squawked in a tiny, high-pitched voice. "What are you doing in my room?"

"It's those silly Polenski children and that green monstrosity," the Reverend proclaimed in too loud a voice. "Now pull yourself together, Anthea! I knew there would be some stupid hoax in all this!"

Middlesex reverted to the opposite end of the vocal range, and a great voice boomed out: "A man of Jesus in a Grand Inquisitors hat! A man of Jesus who wants to punish, not to love. NO! NO! NO!"

"That's not children!" Andrea whispered. "How would they know?"

For once the Reverend had nothing to say.

Middlesex was warming to the role. "Repent, I command, you man of Christ! Love, I say, learn to love. Your Jesus was a man of love."

"Who are you? Where are you? Show yourself - if you dare!" the Reverend Eustace shouted, fingering his dog-collar uneasily. "Show your-self, I say, if you dare!"

Middlesex took a deep breath and then expelled it a maximum velocity through the peep-hole. The whole tapestry shivered.

"When you have learned to love - and start with your poor wife - then will you see me!" Middlesex intoned, lower and more sepulchral than ever.

The Reverend Eustace moved nonchalantly, he hoped, towards the tapestry and then, with a great cry, he pounced. But all he caught was Sagittarius. Middlesex signalled the twins, They all inhaled deeply and blew in unison. Again the tapestry billowed.

"Learn to love – open your heart – learn to love – to love – love..." Middlesex droned hypnotically, letting the sound slowly fade away.

Then a green paw beckoned the twins on. It was time for privacy for the Pilkes. Sergei, however, was reluctant to go, and he did manage to witness Anthea helping a thoroughly shaken man to stamp to death one Grand Inquisitor's hat.

The next set of peep-holes revealed a nursery with Victorian rocking horse, twentieth century train set and Elizabethan hobby-horse. It had an untidy, lived-in look for two of Sir Magnus' grandchildren had only gone home that morning. On the panelled walls, Breughel's picture of Children's Games rubbed shoulders with a Paddington Bear poster and a picture of a space-ship. The room was currently occupied by the Crumbles, halfway through one of their ritual-display arguments. "Look, Martha," Fred Crumble was whining, "the other rooms were nothing - show pieces, guest rooms, but this... this is family! Probably Sir Magnus himself played here when he was young."

"Which is precisely why we shouldn't take any pictures here," Martha argued forcibly. "I believe in the privacy of the individual."

"Then you shouldn't have married a newspaper man," Fred flung back. "Now give me the flash attachment out of your bag."

Martha became icily reasonable and concerned. "Do calm down, Fred. We'll be eating soon, and if you get yourself so steamed up your ulcers are going to give you gyp – especially after that spiced punch! I did warn you not to have any."

Fred groaned and sat down on the old nursing chair, which creaked beneath his weight.

"If you didn't make such a fuss, I wouldn't get so steamed up!"

Middlesex chose that moment to intervene. "Would you please get off my lap," a prim, little voice requested.

Fred looked round startled. "Who was that?"

Martha, busy opening one of the large toy chests, shook her head.

"Would you please get off my lap this instant!" the voice repeated. "This instant, if you please."

Fred jumped up and stared disbelievingly at the chair.

"Thank you so much! Ah, that's more comfortable," purred the little voice.

Fred backed towards his wife. "Can you see anything?" he whispered urgently.

Martha, toy chest forgotten, shook her head again.

"Who are you? Where are you?" Fred asked in a tremulous voice. "Where are you? We want to see you."

"Wanting is not enough," Middlesex replied primly. "If wanting were enough, you would be a loser? No! First you must work hard at believing, then you will see everything!"

"Are you a ghost?" Martha asked bluntly.

"I don't know. Are you?" the prim voice parried.

"You can see me, but I can't see you," Martha shot back logically.

"That is as may be," retorted the voice from the chair. "But you can't see Fred, and Fred can't see you."

"Don't be ridiculous!" Martha's temper flared. "Of course I can see Fred. Can't I, Fred. And Fred can see me."

Middlesex hooted with a spectral laugh of disbelief. "Oh no, no, no! You both see vague shadows labelled Fred and Martha. But you are ghosts one to the other – your inner selves no more visible to each other than I am to you."

"This is preposterous – arguing with an empty chair," Fred shouted. "Who are you? Come on! Show yourself."

Middlesex moaned lightly and primly a couple of times and then intoned: "I am me, who are you... you... you... you?"

The twins were nearly helpless with suppressed giggles at the expressions on the Crumble's faces. Middlesex signalled them to follow him and even Sergei complied immediately. There was really nothing to watch, as Fred and Martha froze into mutual contemplation one of the other.

The final set of peep-holes looked in on a very fine bed-chamber, furnished entirely in the Elizabethan style. A massive four poster bed, with sky-blue hangings emblazoned with Tudor roses in golden thread, dominated the room. There was a writing table and two coffers; a linen fold chest and two square-set upholstered chairs by the great hearth where a log fire crackled and spluttered. The room, like all good Tudor rooms, had a simplicity in which the strength and stability of the carved oaken furniture could be both appreciated and respected. The walls were relieved only by blue damask curtains drawn across the mullioned windows, and by three great tapestries.

The spy holes were to one side of the chimney breast and, when the intrepid trio first looked through, Mrs Polenski and Mrs Cutting were sitting in the armchairs before the fire.

"I wonder if Elizabeth the First ever slept here?" Anna Polenski said, laughing.

"She certainly did sleep around," Susan Cutting said, "in the nicest possible way, of course."

"I like Tudor décor," Anna decided. "It's uncluttered; homely but impressive. I wouldn't mind this as my bedroom."

Captain Polenski had discovered meanwhile a small plaque at the head of the bed. "If you did, you might get more than you bargained for. Listen to this," and he began to read: "This room was used on four occasions between May and October 1541 A. D. by Henry the Eighth, who showed a questionable interest in Catherine de Verte, tenth daughter of Sir Henry de Verte, and who was then seventeen years of age. She died in mysterious circumstances, six months later, and it is reputed that she still visits this room searching for her lover-king."

"Poor child!" Susan Cutting murmured. "What a waste of a life."

Anna shivered. "I know this sounds silly, but I'm getting a distinctive feeling that we're being watched. Let's go - I suddenly don't like it in here anymore."

Dasha was upset at her mother's distress and she attempted to call out to reassure her. She started to call out "Mummy," but Sergei's quick reaction in slapping his hand across her lips, resulted in only a strangulated "Y.. m…" getting through.

All the occupants of Catherine's bedroom heard it, and the Captain said quietly: "Perhaps we're not wanted in here."

Middlesex, sensibly, had decided not to pull any tricks on the Polenskis but G-R-I-D suddenly took over control temporarily. A loud sob followed by a deep sigh drifted across the room as the Captain shepherded his wife and Susan Cutting out of the room. He paused; another sob, another sigh and words seemed to form out of the air: "Oh, my sweet lord... my sweet lord..."

The Captain smiled. "Well played, Middlesex," he murmured to the empty air. "But the Lady Catherine may not like it!" and he went out and shut the door firmly.

Behind the panelling, Middlesex and Sergei dissolved into a gale of laughter but Dasha was uneasy.

"You overdid that," she said reproachfully.

"No harm done," Middlesex crowed. "I'm quite sure the Captain enjoyed the haunting."

"But what about Mum and Mrs Cutting? I think they were really scared."

Middlesex shook a green head confidently. "I think not, but if they did believe it – well, a bit of romance never does harm."

The little passageway now turned sharply to the right, and gave way to a short flight of steps. At the bottom, by the glow of green fur, they could just make out that they were in a small room. They groped around until Sergei knocked over a candle standing on a small table.

"That's a bit of luck," he shouted softly, as he took a cigarette lighter out of his pocket. "I found this lying on a table in the hall, and I thought it might come in handy," he explained as he got the old candle alight.

By its flickering flame, they made out that the walls, floor and arched ceiling were of small Suffolk brick. The remnants of a purple cloth covered a small table, on which was lying another candle and a small silver crucifix.

"It looks like a church," Dasha whispered.

"I bet it's a chapel, a private chapel," Sergei said. "Didn't the Catholics have to have secret ones sometime?"

Then Middlesex noticed an inscribed slab let into the wall at the far end. Dasha took the candle closer and began to decipher it.

"Here lyeth ye mortal remains of Catherine de Verte, beloved tenth daughter and fifteenth child of Henry de Verte and his ladye Anne. May our heavenly Lord forgive our temporal lord and King for ye trespasses he did our name and honore, for we cannot. Buried by the rites of ye true and onlie Church on ye twenty-first day of Aprile 1541 Anno Domini. And may Christ have mercie on her soule."

They stared silently at the stark account of one short life.

"I hope she loved him," Dasha whispered, at last.

"A fat lot of good it did her, even if she did," Sergei retorted.

Middlesex sighed. "How your species likes to torture itself. But come, this is not why we are here."

"It's not?" said Sergei, with mock surprise. "Tell us more, green wizard."

Middlesex did not respond. G-R-A-S-S had taken command and was in no mood for facetiousness. Middlesex held out two green paws.

"Give me your hands, and let your Human Sixth Senses help me. There is something here that we must find out."

Overawed by Middlesex's serious manner, the twins did as they were asked, and waited for what they knew not. Then, slowly, but slowly, a shape seemed to form within the circle, in texture reminiscent of an outline on a piece of tracing paper. There was no colour, but it seemed to be dressed in a long gown with wide sleeves and a girdle, with long tassels, tied around the hips. The chest and neck were covered in fine linen and a wimple adorned the head.

It – she – faced Middlesex, and the twins seemed to hear a flat, translucent voice speaking a language they knew, but of which they could not understand one word. They could only get the drift of the conversation from Middlesex's replies and questions. "You are Matilda, wife to Sir Hubert de Verte und you have come from Normandy... a very good evening to you, my lady... we are the first visitors to this chapel in four hundred years... it is a great honour, my lady... what is it that you would have us tell Sir Magnus?... a sword, a two-edged sword... your late husband's sword... it has been newly walled up in here... oh, it was newly walled up when Sir Henry created this chapel by walling up the far end of the great bread-oven.... yes, yes! We understand you... Sir Magnus should be informed of its existence... yes, I understand, it is his title to the manor... three handspans to the right of the slab and five handspans above the floor.... I will convey your message, my lady... and may you now rest in peace... Farewell, my lady."

Middlesex released the twins hands slowly as the mirage faded. "Why couldn't we understand what she was saying?" Sergei asked quietly.

"It was English as spoken in the last part of the eleventh century," Middlesex replied absent-mindedly. "I had quite forgotten that I could speak it!"

"Did we really see a ghost?" Dasha asked, already unsure of what she had, and had not, seen and heard.

"I think not," Middlesex replied. "But we created one. But come; it is time that we returned to the Great Hall."

Sergei was crestfallen. "But Middlesex, aren't we going to unearth the sword?"

Green authority flooded the little chapel. "No, Sergei, we shall not. That is for Sir Magnus only, should he think it fit so to do. We have afforded the Lady Matilda her peace at last, but her two-edged sword is impotent against attack from the faceless and bloodless bureaucracy of today's world."

"You're not being much fun," Sergei grumbled, as he turned towards the stairs.

"Goodbye, Lady Matilda; goodbye Lady Catherine!" Dasha whispered sadly, as she followed Middlesex and her reluctant brother back into the twentieth century.

CHAPTER XIV

Leave the truth of Itself to the inclination and to the imagination.
(B. O. P. Bk. 3)

When the trio reached the Great Hall, they found the others awaiting them impatiently. Immediately, Sir Magnus asked Middlesex to partner him in to dinner. Then the twins followed, backed by their parents who were discussing secret passages and 'atmospheres' in old buildings. Then came the Reverend Eustace Pilke, hatless now, and his wife with their hands clasped and strange sensations tingling up their respective arms. They were followed by the Cuttings; Jeremiah with a splendid carnation in his buttonhole and Susan with a rare orchid pinned on-to her dress. The Crumbles brought up the rear, each engrossed in the familiar stranger they had just met. The Wizard of Oz, alias Danvers, helped in shepherding in the other guests before joining the guests of honour at the high table. This was a huge, circular affair, laid now with the signs of the zodiac, and lit by scented candles burning inside deep orange mangolda, shining and sculpted to ghoulish heads. At the centre, on a silver dais, was an antique Venetian witches' bowl that splintered the candle-light into myriad rainbows. Small witches rode black serviette broomsticks, and old pewter tableware gleamed dully at each place.

During the scrumptious meal, that was nevertheless meatless in Middlesex's honour, it was only the Polenskis and Susan Cutting who admitted to any 'supernatural' experiences, and the conversation flowed round the cavalcade of people to whom Farthingale Manor had been home.

The Reverend Eustace glowed with an inner warmth that glowed nothing to the excellent wine with which he was being plied. He gazed frequently across at his bright-eyed wife, wondering how he could have been so unresponsive for so long to her gaiety and innocence. He also studied the people round the table, ashamed of former suspicions and uncharitable thoughts – and he laughed as he had not laughed since he was a small child.

Fred Crumble was oblivious of his ulcers and ate heartily. Had his thoughts been on them, he would have marvelled at their sudden tolerance, but his thoughts were on the woman across the table whom he was 'seeing' for the first time. Frequently, his eyes met Martha's and another veil would dissolve between them.

As coffee was served, Middlesex spoke loudly and directly to Sir Magnus.

"May I ask what is known of the Lady Matilda?"

"Which one?" Sir Magnus replied laughing. "It's been a family name right back, and there have been upwards of a dozen of them."

"The first one - the wife of Sir Hubert," Middlesex answered softly, now that all attention was focussed on Sir Magnus.

"Ah, the Lady Matilda from Evreux in Normandy," he exclaimed, as he pierced the end of his exclusive cigar. "She was quite a gal, believe me!"

"Please tell us about her," Dasha begged, "because we–"

"Because we would like to know how it all started," Middlesex broke in loudly.

Sir Magnus glanced swiftly at the twins and Middlesex, before saying slowly, "Yes, I'd be delighted to, and as all good stories begin at the beginning, that is where we will start." He drew deeply on his cigar. "Well, so the legend goes, Sir Hubert was a keen, ambitious knight on the make. So, if he rescued an old woman in distress he made sure she was a rich old woman first. He had plenty of pedigree, claiming descent from the great Viking, Rollo, who had plundered and won Normandy for the Vikings. But as the younger son, of a line of younger sons, who hadn't been all that bright, he was short of money and land."

"Vikings!" Sergei exclaimed. "You mean the Normans were Vikings, really?"

"Yes, most of them were by descent, "Sir Magnus smiled. "The rest were Franks or of mixed blood. Duke William himself was also a descendant of Rollo, but by a more successful line than poor Hubert."

"And come to think of it, you have a Viking name, Sir Magnus," Mrs Polenski observed.

The blue eyes twinkled. *"To go Viking* used to mean 'to raid; to trade; to settle'. I think my family has fulfilled the three conditions; and my family fortune still rests, like the fortune of our society, on the old concept of 'to go viking', albeit in a subtler, more sophisticated way. Yes, I deserve my name!"

Dasha was about to protest that their kind friend was nothing like her concept of a Viking, but Middlesex got there first.

"It is the story of your species, Sir Magnus, which is now being extended to space itself. But let us return to more simple times - or so they appear at this distance!"

Sir Magnus smiled; and picked up the threads of his saga: "Our young Sir Hubert was looking for a fortune, as I was saying, and he was in the service of a certain elderly roue, Sir Rolande de Beauchamps. This gentleman, decided on the death of his third wife, to marry a young heiress and repair the family fortune, which he had squandered during his life." Sir Magnus paused to sip at his brandy. "Now, fortunately for him," he went on, "he had, many years before, saved the life of the Count of d'Arbreville in a brawl and so, when he made representations to the Count for the hand and considerable dowry of his sixteen-year old daughter, the Count could hardly refuse. Now, our bright young man, Sir Hubert, was dispatched to bring the hapless girl to her new lord and master. Of course they fell immediately in love; the fact that she also carried a great dowry with her person did nothing to dampen Sir Hubert's ardour!"

Dasha felt cold fingers clenching at her stomach. Here were all the ingredients for tragedy.

"So the cavalcade came riding up to Rolande's castle by the River Seine. The eager bridegroom climbed up to the battlements to catch a sight of his new bride. There he leant against some masonry which had only just been reset; it gave way under his ponderous weight, and he plunged down into the moat. The shock, and the length of time he was in the stinking water – for neither he nor his retainers could swim – resulted in pneumonia, and he was dead by cock-crow a day later."

There was a general sigh of relief around the table. "And what happened then?" Sergei asked impatiently.

"Well, my young friend," Sir Magnus went on obligingly, "what happened then is that the young couple dared to grasp the chance that fate had granted them, with both bands. So that by the time Matilda returned to her father, she was far enough gone with child for him to reluctantly agree to the marriage, on half-dowry of course, of his favourite daughter to a penniless knight."

"Were they happy?" Dasha asked wistfully.

"That I don't know," Sir Magnus smiled and sipped again at his brandy. "But I do know that when she joined her husband here, in his new fortified Manor House – a reward from the victorious King, alias Duke, William – she brought with her six sons and five daughters!"

"Eleven children!" Sergei shouted. "Why, that's a football side!"

"But she didn't look..." Dasha began rashly, but Middlesex cut her short again.

"Please go on, Sir Magnus. How did things go with them here?"

"I suppose they settled down to their new life well enough, but then came the day when Sir Hubert needed to make a trip back to Normandy. He went alone, leaving Matilda in charge here. But he never got there, because his ship was wrecked in a storm in the Channel. The eldest son, Edwin, was only eleven at the time – apparently the three eldest children were all girls – so Matilda set about holding his birthright until he was of age. And that was no mean task in those days, I assure you."

"Did she ever use–" It was Sergei being reckless this time, but again Middlesex interrupted.

"And was she successful, Sir Magnus?"

"Indeed she was," Sir Magnus laughed, very aware of the tension between the twins and Middlesex. "It was said that Sir Hubert left her his two-edged sword, and that the Lady Matilda could wield it as effectively as any man – and that she did so on more than one occasion."

"I thought women then were all weak and soppy," Sergei protested.

"No, no," Sir Magnus smiled. "They were tough times, and the women were tough too. They wouldn't have survived if they hadn't been. And, in any case, Viking women were pretty emancipated, with many rights and freedoms."

"Is that really so?" the Captain voiced the general surprise.

"Yes," Sir Magnus said firmly. "It was a combination of Christianity, the Crusades, and chivalry that demoted women to mere chattels in the centuries following the Conquest. But our Matilda was in the Viking tradition and she held on to, and ruled her lands with, an iron hand."

Dasha and Sergei, trying to recall the shadowy figure in the chapel, found it hard to reconcile the two versions of the Lady Matilda. Except, Sergei thought, she had been stubborn enough to hang around for nearly a thousand years to pass on the secret of the sword.

Sir Magnus continued his story. "But the Lady Matilda was uneasy about her eldest son, Edwin. He seemed to her, apparently, too gentle to hold on to his birthright. So, in accordance with the custom of those times when inheritance, though following the blood-line, wasn't automatically to the eldest, she hid their father's sword. Then she informed her five sons that whoever should find it would be the new Lord of the Manor."

"It sounds like a version of Excalibur," the Reverend remarked.

"But what about the girls?" Dasha demanded. "I thought they had rights too."

"So they did," Sir Magnus answered. "But they could not inherit directly, though inheritance could pass through them to their sons. So the hunt was on, and a year later, the second son, William – quite a bully boy, by all accounts – found the sword and became the new Lord when he was seventeen."

"What happened to Edwin?" Sergei asked eagerly. "Did William kill him?"

"No," Sir Magnus replied. "He entered a monastery, and eventually became its abbot. And so, until the Reformation, the heir to Farthingale was always so chosen if there was more than one son. I think it must have been inheritance of the fittest, because at no time did the fortunes of the manor go into decline. Rather the reverse!"

"What happened at the Reformation then?" asked Mrs Polenski.

Sir Magnus shrugged his shoulders. "Somewhere in the house there is supposed to be a small secret chapel, because the de Verte's of that time stuck to the old faith. All of them, that is, except the eldest son, who enjoyed life at court and found the sacrifice of his faith an acceptable price to pay. When the king got interested in one of the girls, Catherine – perhaps you saw the plaque in the Tudor bedroom – old Sir Henry deemed it wise to pack his other four sons off to relatives in France. Before they left, he cheated and told the second son that the sword was hidden in the chapel. Six months later, they were both dead. Sir Henry of a broken heart, it was said, over the dishonouring of Catherine, and his second son of smallpox. So, the eldest son, being on the winning side; inherited without the sword, and the Manor has been passed on in the orthodox way ever since."

"Would you like to find the chapel, and the sword?" Sergei asked eagerly.

"Personally, I doubt the whole story, and certainly the chapel has never been found," Sir Magnus replied non-committally.

"But would you like to find it?" Dasha was insistent.

Sir Magnus studied his cigar, then glanced briefly at the twins and Middlesex before answering briskly, "No, I don't believe I would. There is much truth in the idea that what one does not own completely, one cannot lose completely. No, I think it is better this way."

Suddenly the Wizard of Oz stood up. "It is five minutes to twelve, Sir Magnus. It is time for the entertainment."

Sir Magnus rose to his feet. "Ladies and gentlemen!" he called loudly. "The witching hour is upon us. If you would please follow me..."

With excitement, the guests trooped out and went quickly down into the Great Hall, which was now in darkness save for the light from the fire. Then the grandfather clock began to chime the hour and silence fell. On the second stroke, four laser beams sprang to life and created, out of their energy, a three-dimensional witch which rode the air around the great candelabra. She was joined by skeletons and ghoulies which appeared out of nothingness and disappeared into nothingness. Low-pitched cackling laughter spiced with wails, shrieks and screams awoke, in the modern minds of the spectators, ancient dreads and forebodings.

In the minstrels' gallery, a group of uninvited but perennial guests at Hallowe'en festivities were manifestly concerned. Once it had been the monopoly of a higher authority than scientists and electronic trickery, for revelations to come in a flash of blinding light. Here, indeed, was a vision to haunt beings caught in the limbo between being and non-being. The vibrations of their distress aroused G-R-A-S-S, and Middlesex responded immediately. Flexing the powerful haunches, Itself joined them in the gallery at the sixth stroke of the witching hour. Then the intensity of a green glow vied with the holographic illusions and, to the watchers below, it appeared that a concourse of a thousand years of history was assembled in that one small place. There stood the Lady Matilda holding aloft the mighty two-edged sword; the gentle Edwin in monk's garb and the Lady Catherine large with child; the court gentleman with ruffs, cloak and earring, jostled by crinolined ladies and bewigged men; by Regency dandies and Puritan girls; by an ermine-cloaked judge and youngsters in the uniforms of the First and Second World Wars. Of other worlds, of other times, but they were all entitled to bathe in the green glow, for they were all de Vertes.

Then the great grandfather clock chimed the twelfth stroke and on the instant, the lasers died. The Great Hall flashed into electric life and, in the musician's gallery, a normal, five-foot Green Rabbit gazed down alone at the astounded company.

Then, stamping one strong hind leg, Itself threw green paws up in a theatrical gesture. "Sir Magnus, my friends – the future belongs to us all. This house is a ship that sails the centuries, carrying a cargo of spirits, of all those who have lived, and loved and died here. And you and I, my friends, are also ships, carrying the past into the future!" The pause which followed this dramatic announcement was a mistake – if it had been Middlesex's intention to continue with the oration. Sergei, as always rather irritated when Middlesex became philosophical, began to clap as he shouted loudly, "And may God bless all who sail in us!"

Over the laughter which followed, Sir Magnus called for champagne, declaring it was high time they launched themselves. Then glass in hand, he went up to the Musician's Gallery.

"My friend, you found the chapel and the sword, didn't you?" he asked quietly.

Middlesex nodded. "We met the Lady Matilda, and she asked us to inform you of its location. She has forgone her rest these thousand years, so that a de Verte might know."

"Then you shall write it down and it shall be sealed into the Family Archive Box," said Sir Magnus solemnly. "But I have no need of it!" Then he went to the edge of the balcony and called out loudly, lifting his champagne glass. "My friends, I give you a toast. I give you Middlesex – a right CAPITAL spirit!"

Dasha and Sergei, tasting the first bubbly of their lives, shouted louder than anyone else. "To Middlesex – a right CAPITAL spirit."

Middlesex bowed solemnly before turning to young Tubble and whispering a request in his ear. With a loud cry of, "I'm in the mood for a cha-cha!" Itself leapt down from the balcony and landed by the twins. Within seconds, a laughing, singing snake wound its tipsy way up and down corridors and stairways; a long line of carefree humans following a Green Rabbit, twirling the silver-capped ebony stick with the expertise of a major dome. Finally, Itself led them out through the great studded doors into the frosty moonlight for a quick spin round the circular driveway. After which, in the warmth of the Great Hall, the party went on, far into the small hours of All Souls Day.

Only the Reverend Pilke and Andrea left early, for he had a wife to love and a sermon to rewrite for the day's services.

It was nearly noon before WORLD'S END stirred into action. Over breakfast, the twins and Middlesex recounted their adventure in the chapel, confessed to their haunting prank in the Tudor bedroom and apologised to Mrs Polenski.

"That's alright," the Captain said comfortably, a wicked gleam in his eye "Because what you couldn't know, because you couldn't see it, was what was going on in the alcove on the other side of the fire-place."

"What was going on?" Sergei demanded suspiciously.

"Well, there was a perfect example of a Tudor rocking cradle," his father explained. "And last night, I would swear that it was rocking gently, all by itself!"

"Did you see Lady Catherine's ghost too?" Dasha asked breathlessly.

"Stefan, stop teasing," his wife laughed. "You know quite well that there were no ghosts!"

"But there were, Mum," Sergei shouted loudly. "We saw the Lady Matilda in the little chapel!"

Middlesex coughed delicately. "No, Sergei. We were in the chapel, but we created the ghost."

"How do you mean, Middlesex?" a puzzled Mrs Polenski asked. "You created a ghost?"

"We created her," Middlesex explained, "as a television set creates sounds and pictures from the otherwise undetectable radio waves."

"You mean she's there all the time?" asked an incredulous Sergei.

"All things are eternally present," Middlesex stated with finality. "But we are not switched on to all things, all of the time."

"But what evidence have you for asserting that you know that all things are eternally present?" the Captain argued.

"How do we know that radio waves are passing through this room all the time?" his wife asked rhetorically. "We only know by turning on an instrument that can receive and interpret them. The same with the cosmic waves that are pinging through us at this moment. Yes, I take your point, Middlesex – I think!"

Middlesex nodded, and began again, "Now take an ant, for instance."

"No thank you, I'd rather not," Sergei giggled.

"Take an ant," Middlesex repeated, ignoring the interruption. "It has sight and hearing, but it cannot see or hear the wholeness of, say, a motorcar in the way in which we can."

"Maybe not," the Captain argued, "but it can explore it by crawling into every nook and cranny of the thing."

"And it still cannot experience it as a whole," Middlesex parried. "Nor its latent power and function. Just so, the higher intelligences crawl over their world but see no more of total reality, of its power and function, than the ant of the car."

"But the ant has its own sense of reality," the Captain objected.

"As have all species," Middlesex conceded. "But each reality is only a part of the whole, and the sum total only still a part of the ultimate reality. But it is true that there are times when we break in, or are broken into, by other realities."

"Sounds crazy to me, man!" Sergei shouted impatiently. "I knows what I see!"

"True," Middlesex shouted. "But you also sees what you know! And when you've worked out that little conundrum, you'll be as crazy as the rest of us!"

"Well, I know that's it's twelve-thirty and I want to go out," Sergei stated flatly. "Come on, Middlesex, or the day will be gone. Let's go up the airfield."

"When you've done the washing up, dear," his mother ordered firmly, "Because I know I shall see the reality of Sir Magnus and Danvers coming up the garden path at precisely seven-thirty for dinner."

The afternoon was spent revisiting the scene of the first Middlesex escapade in the old hangars on the airfield. They walked across stubble fields awaiting the plough, and stopped to pick late blackberries in the sprawling hedgerows. The air sparkled over a landscape, heedful of the warning of frosty nights, preparing to go into suspended animation against the hostility of winter. In the blue-mist distance trees, in varying degrees of readiness, linked earth to sky with the still dark green of the oak and ash; the brown-yellow splay of chestnut and the bared willow and poplar. And everywhere, warm rays of the slanted sun encouraged belief in the spring to come.

Frequently, Middlesex stopped to sniff the harvest-purged air, to mark the passing of a small creature by pawmarks in the soft ground, or simply to exclaim, "splendid, just CAPITAL, splendid!" The twins urged their friend on, played tag and grew impatient.

Suddenly, the green haunches flexed and a wild, green creature bowled over them towards the hangars.

"Come on, slow coaches, Let's be having that kite then!"

When the twins caught up, breathless and giggling, Sergei handed over the aerodynamic kite which they had bought the previous Saturday. Within minutes, Middlesex had it up, performing acrobatics, with consummate ease.

"Come, fly with me!" Itself sang out loudly, getting the kite even higher.

Thereafter, the three of them took it in turns, each trying to out-skill the others. The twins, however, could not sustain the pull on the strings to the height of which Middlesex was capable. At one point, Sergei ran home for more string, and came back with a bag of cakes and celery as well. Now Middlesex coaxed the kite to a much greater height, and the twins became worried. That kite represented, after all, a great deal of their combined pocket money!

"Bring it down a bit," Sergei shouted. "I want a go!"

Middlesex nodded assent, but the moment later – without warning as its sound waves trailed behind it, out of nowhere it seemed a jet fighter plane zoomed low over them. On a NATO exercise, and on a liberal interpretation by the reckless pilot of two hundred feet on his altimeter, the plane seemed to skim at tree height. It climbed, circled and hurtled back across the airfield, screaming its message of destruction. Sergei and Dasha put their hand over their ears and instinctively ducked. Middlesex, holding the kite with maximum strength, yelled, "Watch it, old chap, watch it!"

The kite strings snapped, collapsed and trailed to earth as the plane's wing cut straight through them. The plane shot up and roared out of sight. As the twins looked up again, they saw their precious kite spiralling upwards like a mad thing in the whirlpool of air created by the jet.

"Oh, Middlesex, what's happened?" Dasha shouted, near to tears, running towards the trailing strings.

"Your kite is now a free agent," Middlesex shouted back. "That maniac cut the strings!"

They watched helplessly as the kite's gyrations slowed and it began its plunge back to earth. They chased it, exertion sapping their anger, and finally were relieved to see it coming down over the hedge round WORLD'S END.

Sergei reached it first, lying among the bronze chrysanthemums. He bent to pick it up when his eye was attracted by something glinting on the soil. He picked it up, and brushed at the bits of soil to discover that it was a silver button off a policeman's jacket.

"It must have got ripped off when they charged through the hedge after Middlesex," Dasha said, laughing at the find.

They looked at the impenetrable bramble hedge at the rear of the flower bed and shuddered with pity for the Constables.

"They must've been pretty desperate," said Sergei.

"Middlesex does tend to have that effect on one!" remarked the Captain drily, who had just come out to see what all the noise was about. "Now, come and see the light I've rigged up in Middlesex's hidey-hole."

As they walked into the house, Middlesex turned to Sergei smugly. "Treasure that moment of my first night here, Sergei! G-R-I-L."

"Oh, don't start that load of codswallop again," he interrupted crossly, but he had to admit to himself that it was all rather strange how it had all worked out. "I think it was H-A-S-S and not G-R-A-S-S at work, anyway!" he added, his good humour returning.

On the stroke of seven-thirty, Mrs Polenski did see Sir Magnus and Danvers walking up the garden path. Over dinner, Sir Magnus revealed that he and Danvers had spent the day delving into his family archives.

"I have found out quite a lot about your Adam Smith," he announced, "And you, dear friend," he addressed Middlesex, "are going to be tickled green!"

Mrs Polenski finished serving out the apple and blackberry pie, and then settled down to listen.

"It would appear," Sir Magnus began, pouring a liberal helping of cream onto his pie, "that Sir Magnus the third – I am the fourteenth, by the way – who inherited in 1441 had tastes both expensive and adventurous. Around 1446, he took off on one of the Crusades. He left his young wife, Isabelle, to look after their four young children and the Manor. When he returned, nearly three years later, he brought back a lot of loot and a Cornish man, by the name of Adam, in his entourage."

"Our Adam!" exclaimed Dasha.

Sir Magnus nodded. "So it would seem. A house was then built for this Cornish man; this house at the cost of £75, which was a lot in those days. Finally, to bind him morally to the family and ensure his trust-worthiness with the precious metals, I imagine, he was married off to a young ward of Sir Magnus. Her name was Eleanor and it would seem that she was his orphaned niece and quite penniless – her only asset lying in her very nimble fingers when it came to embroidery, and she worked on many hangings for the house in later years." Sir Magnus leant back comfortably. "I think Magnus the third must have found himself a very special whitesmith, to have treated him so lavishly."

"Do you think Adam and Eleanor loved each other?" Dasha asked.

"I don't know," Sir Magnus smiled. "There is no record of that in our ledgers. But I hope that they did."

"What does it matter anyway?" Sergei said unsympathetically. "What happened then?"

"All we know," Danvers picked up the narrative, having finished his dessert, "is that Adam was supplied with gold and silver in quite considerable quantities over the years, and produced tableware and ornaments for the family. And, yes, he made many things for the church too. Some silver bells, a great rarity, and altar plates, candlesticks, crucifixes and things like that."

"They were the ones, no doubt, that were melted down, unhappily, during the Civil War – except for the bells which, reputedly, were buried, although they have never been found," Sir Magnus added. "As you probably know, the de Vertes were Royalists, and they made big donations to the King's fight against Parliament."

"But what else do you know about Adam and Eleanor?" Dasha asked impatiently.

"Very little, except that he worked here until he died – and then his son carried on," Danvers told her.

Sir Magnus laughed. "But it may interest you to know, and you in particular, Mrs Polenski, that when the gallant Sir Magnus went off to foreign fields again some ten years, and eight children later, Adam was ordered to make silver girdles, with locks, for the Lady Isabelle and the two eldest girls. Whether these were a refined type of chastity belt, I don't know."

"Were there any more children, or did Sir Magnus mislay the key?" she laughed back.

"She died before her husband returned," Danvers answered. "And the two girls were packed off to be nuns."

"A very neat solution!" the Captain commented. "Perhaps that ties in with the books in our hidey hole, which I was glancing through this afternoon. There's a whole inventory there, too, of work done – including one about a clasp for a cloak done by the young Adam for the Ladye Marye. It lists it as being a Lover's Knot done, and I quote, '*to mine own devizing and done in silver of my owne purchasing.*' The date was 1456, I think."

"Do you think he was in love with the lady Mary?" Dasha was eager for yet more romance. "How terrible if they were in love, and she was sent off to a convent."

Sergei snorted. "You're so soppy, Dasha. Everybody's got to love everybody else when you're around."

"And you just pretend to be a toughie," Dasha shot back. "But you're not really. You're just being dishonest!"

"And you are both small ants exploring the motor that powers your human emotions," Middlesex cut in, referring to the conversation at the breakfast table. "But hopefully, your perception will grow until you will be able to perceive the latent power and function of those emotions."

Sergei, hurt by what seemed to him a public betrayal by Middlesex, flung back, "Like you do, I suppose!"

"Yes, like I do" Middlesex replied wistfully, torn between sadness for and elation at the human race. "But then I am not of your species!"

After dinner, the party went into the hidey-hole in twos and threes, to explore it by the light of the Captain's 'electrickery'. They examined the ancient ledgers, which were written first in the hand of Adam Senior and then in that of his son. The third book came to an abrupt end half-way through, where a different hand had written:

"This daye, being the fourteenth of June in the 25th of our Sovereign lord and King Henry Eight 1536 Anno Domini, dyed Adam Smith, whitesmith to our lord Sir Henry de Verte in the 76th yeare of his age to heaven.

This daye, also, be this room walled up by ordere of the said Sir Henry, on feare of the wroth of our Sovereign Lord the King.

Consummatum Est."

"That was just five years before the Lady Catherine died," Dasha exclaimed when she read it.

"I think that my family must have hung on to their possessions by the skin of their elder son's teeth," Sir Magnus laughed. "All the same, the king did manage to extract his revenge, did he not?"

Dasha nodded, as she replied: "But I'm glad they held on through everything, or you wouldn't be here with me now. Or Middlesex either probably. G-R-A-S-S must have known about this, you know, and that's why Middlesex came here!"

"You may well be right, my dear," said Sir Magnus. "And thank you for the compliment of valuing my presence. And you know, if it hadn't been for another tyrant, Hitler, you wouldn't be here for our delight!"

When they returned to the lounge, they found the others waiting for them in their coats.

"What's happening? Are we going out somewhere?" Dasha called with excitement.

"Middlesex wants us all to walk down to the junction and wave *au revoir*," her mother answered quietly.

"You're not going away again yet!" Dasha cried. "Oh, not yet, please, Middlesex."

Middlesex took her hands between green paws, and held her gaze.

"The time is ripe. G-R-A-S-S dictates, and G-R-I-L insists. But we shall meet again before too long."

As the dark, velvet eyes soothed her mind, Dasha found that acceptance came easily, naturally. "I'll just get coats for Sir Magnus and me," she said quietly.

Then the little party walked out into the frosty moonlight.

Middlesex sniffed the nostalgic scents of autumn and green ears became taut. They grew sensitive to the pulse of that other world of night, and the green glow gained power.

Sergei and Dasha walked, one to each side, linking green arms.

The adults walked behind, and laughter filled the lane as Middlesex started off, and the twins and Danvers joined in, their private nursery rhyme. For the encore, Sir Magnus added his rich baritone, and the Captain and Mrs Polenski loudly clapped the rhythm with gloved hands. A third rendition brought them to the one-armed signpost, and Middlesex walked onto the grass verge alone and stood by it.

"What was it you told me at our first meeting, Dasha?" Itself asked softly. "That a By Road is a little road that is not often used?"

"Did I?" Dasha asked uncertainly.

"You did," Middlesex asserted, "And it is true and it is sad, for it is down the By Roads in this world that our dreams lie…"

"Where are you going this time, and when are you coming back?" shouted Sergei, in no mood for one of the Green Rabbit discourses. He would have been prepared to keep Middlesex from going by force, if such a thing had been possible. As it was not, and he knew that it was not, impotence made him casual.

"You will create me again, or I shall create you, when G-R-I-L and G-R-A-S-S deem the time is ripe," Middlesex declared cheerily.

"And together, we will create the world again. But for now, *au revoir* my friends – and may your world be green, always."

As the oration ended, the great haunches flexed, and the green glow bounded away in a madly erratic course across mist-swathed fields. All was hushed and still in the cold moonscape. Six pairs of eyes watched the receding glow, yet not one of the six pairs of lips could frame any word of farewell. How could they say *au revoir*, even, to that which was with them still?

0 - 0 - 0 - 0 - 0 - 0 - 0

www.ingramcontent.com/pod-product-compliance
Lightning Source LLC
Chambersburg PA
CBHW060119260626
47160CB00005B/1936